Dear Readers,

It's a new year—so why not resolve to make more time for romance? With four brand-new novels from Bouquet, you're off to a great start!

We kick off this month with talented Vanessa Grant. When an astronomer attends her high-school reunion, she's not looking for love—until she meets the man who was once the town bad boy. Soon they're **Seeing Stars**—together! And in Marcia Evanick's final installment of the Wild Rose series, **Jeremiah's Return** is the last thing one woman expects to provide a breathtaking chance at passion . . . and love.

Rising star Carol Rose is back with **Risky Business,** the funny, sexy story of a sham engagement—which becomes all too real when a straitlaced businessman realizes the wild-at-heart photographer in on the charade is the only woman he's ever wanted. Finally, talented newcomer Sara Howard presents the story of a woman scouting Wyoming locations for a movie—and finds her **Fantasy Man** instead!

Here's to a new year full of laughs and love. Enjoy!

Kate Duffy
Editorial Director

TROUBLE INCARNATE

When his boss had invited him to dinner, he had known what it meant. His hard work and long hours had gained him some notice. The subdued clink of cutlery and the murmur of cultured voices met Josh as he turned the corner into the main room. His steps quickened as he caught sight of Dave Williams across the room.

He faltered a second later when his gaze swept the table's other occupants. To Dave's right sat his wife, and beyond her was . . . Katie Flanagan?

Josh stared.

Was Katie Flanagan really sitting there next to his boss?

Katie sat at the table, a teasing smile on her luscious lips and triumph in her blue eyes. A black knit dress clung to her curves, baring her throat and shoulders to the gleaming candlelight. With her red-gold hair in a cloud around her shoulders and mischief in her eyes, she looked like trouble incarnate.

Every muscle in Josh's body felt clenched. Everything he'd worked for, everything he craved was on the line tonight. Katie had threatened to try and destroy him if he didn't renegotiate the loan on the studio. He had known better than to hope she'd just go away.

Josh forced a smile onto his face.

"Darling," Katie said as she stretched out a welcoming hand.

Well aware that the others were observing, Josh thrust aside his confusion and took her slender hand in his, not resisting when she pulled him down for a kiss. The satin texture of her lips and the warm rush of her breath sent his heart rate up several notches. It was the merest of salutes, a polite brushing of lips, but it left Josh feeling he'd burst into flames.

Very few people got to him like Katie Flanagan.

RISKY
BUSINESS

Carol Rose

ZEBRA BOOKS
Kensington Publishing Corp.

http://www.zebrabooks.com

ZEBRA BOOKS are published by

Kensington Publishing Corp.
850 Third Avenue
New York, NY 10022

All Kensington Titles, Imprints and Distributed Lines are available at special quantity discounts for bulk purchases for sales promotions, premiums, fund raising, educational or institutional use.

Special book excerpts or customized printings can also be created to fit specific needs. For details, write or phone the office of the Kensington special sales manager: Kensington Publishing Corp., 850 Third Avenue, New York, NY 10022, attn: Special Sales Department, Phone: 1-800-221-2647.

Zebra, the Z logo, and Bouquet Reg. U.S. Pat. & TM Off.

First Printing: January, 2001
10 9 8 7 6 5 4 3 2 1

Printed in the United States of America

In loving memory of
Barbara Hagood Allred
who left this world
too soon and whose gentle smile
I will always miss

One

Katie Flanagan couldn't let Josh Morgan take her grandfather's photography studio. Grandpa may have been dead these past seven years, but in her heart he remained the one stalwart figure of her childhood. Surely Josh couldn't be serious about foreclosing. While he'd always been stuffy, she had never thought him mean-spirited.

Her heart shifted into overdrive as Katie nervously crossed the threshold into Josh's office.

He stood behind a large desk, his hair as dark as she remembered, his eyes the same impossible blue. Two years ago, he'd been a young executive on the rise, a sexy, arrogant force to be reckoned with.

At a first glance, it didn't look as if that had changed. Even his office with its array of computer equipment and the deferential secretary sitting outside proclaimed his status as a major player in the business world.

Assistant vice president.

The power suit he wore did nothing to hide his broad shoulders, either. Funny how she remembered some things so vividly. When he'd been briefly engaged to her older sister, Erin, Katie had found Josh Morgan both amusing and irritating. His occasionally stuffy conservatism had often set the spark to her too-ready temper.

But his current classy surroundings and big job title didn't surprise her. Josh had been on the way up when she'd first met him three years ago. He'd always been driven to succeed.

She'd come here this morning optimistically hoping that he'd put the events of the past behind him and gone on with his life.

"Josh!" A tumble of joy coursing through her, Katie strode forward fully intending to give him a hug. To her surprise, she realized she'd missed sparring with him.

"Katie Flanagan?" Josh blurted out, looking thunderstruck as he stood behind his desk.

"Yes! It's me." She gave him a congratulatory smile as she skidded to a halt in front of the desk, deciding to forego the hug for now.

"You got the foreclosure notice," he concluded grimly, nothing close to enthusiasm on his face.

She supposed that was to be expected since they'd had no contact for the last couple of years. Not since Erin ran off with his brother, not even bothering to inform Josh of the fact. It was the most thoughtless thing she'd ever known her sister to do, especially considering how Josh had stepped in and offered to marry Erin when she'd found herself pregnant by a previous lover.

As loyal to her sister as she was, Katie didn't think calling in to a radio talk show and spilling the whole story actually constituted as "informing" a man when his fiancée was eloping with his own brother.

Josh had a right to be angry about the whole situation, but Katie wasn't letting him punish her and the studio for something Erin and Josh's brother had done. Though she understood Josh had to have been crushed by their betrayal. Who wouldn't have been?

And then there was the money he'd loaned to Erin to resurrect Grandpa's studio. When Erin defaulted on the payments six months ago, it must've felt like insult added to injury.

But Katie had responsibility for neither of those offenses and she couldn't let him foreclose on the studio.

"I got some kind of legal-looking letter," she told him cheerfully. "Aren't you going to invite me to sit down?"

"There's no point," he said abruptly, his expression less than welcoming. "We have nothing to discuss."

"Yes, of course, we do." Katie sat down in a chair facing his desk. "This whole studio loan problem."

He remained standing. "You haven't bothered yourself about the loan for the last six months when no payments were being made."

"I only found out about Erin dropping the payments three months ago." She leaned forward eagerly. "But now I have this great idea."

"Good for you. It can't have anything to do with me."

"Just listen," she insisted. "This is the best plan. It solves all our problems."

With every appearance of reluctance, Josh lowered himself into the leather chair behind his desk.

"Our problems?"

"When Erin left town two years ago, she closed down the studio and dropped the keys off with me, just like that, and I didn't think anything more about it."

"Very Flanagan-like," Josh sneered, his fingers drumming against the arm of the chair.

He wasn't being the least bit friendly, Katie reflected, wisely choosing not to confront him about it. She might be a tad impulsive at times, but she had to convince him to change his mind about the loan. There was no sense in getting him riled up by pointing out his negative attitude.

"Anyway," Katie forged ahead. "Your letter got me to thinking. I've decided to run the studio myself. I think it might be my niche. I took a photography class in high school and won an award! The studio needs some work, though. The building is rundown, some of the equipment needs replacing, but I don't think it'll take me long to whip it into shape."

She sent her most optimistic smile across the desk. "So I was hoping you could help me."

"Help you?" he snorted. "You want me to do what exactly?"

"Well, it's not like you'll be out any *more* money," Katie said quickly, her hope of that exact thing dying a swift death. "Just give me time to get the studio together and going before I start paying off the money we owe you."

A smile curled the corners of Josh's mouth as he leaned his head back against his chair and started laughing. The full, rich sound filled the room, eventually diminishing into masculine chuckles. "You have a lot of nerve, Katie Flanagan. You've never been short on nerve."

"I kind of hoped you'd moved beyond all the stuff that happened with Erin," she murmured, not sure whether or not she should be encouraged by his laughter.

"I'm sure you did," he agreed, a decidedly unfriendly grin on his face.

"After all, it's not like you guys were really engaged," she pointed out.

"Regardless of what prompted our relationship, I was stupid enough to genuinely offer to marry Erin," Josh corrected her grimly.

"Then she miscarried and met your brother . . ."

"And the rest is history," he finished with a sarcastic smile.

"Yes, but all that has nothing to do with the studio, and my taking it over is a great idea. I don't know why I didn't think of it before." She edged forward in her chair.

"If you want to start a photography studio, go get a loan," Josh said with brutal indifference.

She made a face at him. "I talked to one loan officer at a bank, but he kept getting hung up on my lack of experience. It's like all my weekends of helping Grandpa don't count for anything."

"And you have no collateral." Josh laughed.

"Nothing but the studio and you hold a loan against that," she agreed reluctantly, her temper starting to simmer. After all, *she* wasn't the one who dumped him!

"You're a bad risk," he concluded with apparent satisfaction.

"That's what he said," she admitted, pushing her annoyance aside with an eye on the main goal. "So I thought maybe you and I could come to some kind of terms."

He chuckled again. "You must be kidding. Your sister runs off with my brother after I offered to marry her to give her child a name. She doesn't even bother to tell me face-to-face—and you think I'm going to give you, her flighty younger sister, the opportunity to screw me over again?"

"It was a long time ago," Katie said desperately. "And

it really had nothing to do with me. I wasn't the one who dumped you."

"No, you were a bystander. A typical Flanagan who didn't have the moral courage to tell me when your sister started cheating on me," he retorted.

Katie bit back a defensive retort, aware of being on shaky ground. Maybe it hadn't been her business to report her sister's deceit, but she knew she hadn't kept quiet out of loyalty alone. If she were honest with herself, she had to admit she couldn't stand the idea of Josh married to Erin.

They were wrong for each other, as subsequent circumstances had proved.

Was he married now? she wondered.

Glancing over, Katie scanned his ringless hand. Of course, some married men didn't wear rings.

"But it's not just the past," Josh leaned forward. "Even if I didn't have reason to hate the entire Flanagan family, I still choose my financial risks more carefully these days. And you don't have a particularly commendable history yourself."

"What do you mean by that?" Katie said hotly.

"From what I've heard, you've been busy the last few years, living the same sort of irresponsible, self-centered life your mother and sister live."

"I don't know what you're talking about!"

"Let's see. You're twenty-four and working as what? A waitress. At a different restaurant every three months. You've taken junior college classes with at least five different majors that I know of and you've been engaged twice. You dumped both guys, and left the last one actually standing at the altar."

"There's nothing wrong with being a waitress! And it wasn't my fault that I got hives when I thought about marrying Doug. You don't know anything about it! And I didn't deliberately leave Rick standing at the altar. I tried to call him before the ceremony, but his machine wasn't working," she declared, her temper rising.

The way Josh put it, she sounded like a flake, but it wasn't true at all.

Here it was—Josh's ugly stuffed shirt tendency.

"And how do you know all this anyway? You're just listening to gossip," Katie declared righteously.

"You forget," he said with sarcasm. "Your sister is still living with my brother, on and off. He keeps in touch with my aunt and she's not likely to spread unfounded rumors."

"Still, there were many extenuating circumstances that you know nothing about." Katie sat back in the chair, raising her chin.

"What I know is that avoidance is your family motto. No Flanagan ever lives up to her commitments. Your father only showed up half a dozen times in your life and your mother has been married and divorced six times. If it hadn't been for your grandfather, the state probably would have taken you and Erin away from your mother."

"My mother did the best she could," Katie defended. "And that's all ancient history."

"Maybe so," he concluded, "but I have put the insanity of my association with your family behind me. Far, far behind me."

Josh leaned forward, his eyes flinty and his voice grim. "I don't even want anyone to know that I was ever foolish enough to be involved with a Flanagan. This is my deep, dark secret. I am a sane, rational, fairly intelligent man.

My Flanagan period could do nothing but besmirch the reputation I've worked to build."

"You're just being vindictive," she retorted, as disappointed in him as she was angry. "It's the radio talk show thing, isn't it? You're mad about Erin calling that disc jockey and talking about dumping you in front of thousands of people. You still haven't gotten over the embarrassment, even though you were never specifically identified."

He snorted, pushing away from his desk to stand. "We don't have anything else to discuss."

"Maybe I should call that radio station now and give them the rest of the story. Tell them how you were the guy Erin talked about leaving and now you're foreclosing on me out of spite," Katie challenged, her impulsive tongue taking on a life of it's own.

"Don't be ridiculous," he said, annoyed.

"Don't *you* be ridiculous. You can't foreclose on the studio. It's my heritage and I'll do whatever I have to do to keep it."

"Are you threatening me?" His eyes narrowed.

Katie jumped to her feet, her heart pounding. "If I have to. I've just got to get the studio going and I don't think it's too much to ask you to give me some time."

"You want me to hold the note on this harebrained scheme and then pull your butt out of the fire when it fails," he said in grim conclusion.

"I'm not going to fail!" she yelled. "I've never been more serious about anything in my life."

The door behind her opened suddenly and Katie swiveled around, glaring at the intruder.

"Josh, we need to go over . . ." A thirty-something guy

in a suit came to a halt just inside the door. The man's gaze immediately strayed in Katie's direction, an appreciative expression slipping onto his face as his scrutiny dropped to her short, tight skirt.

"I'm sorry, I didn't know you were busy," he said to Josh, a smirk spreading across his face.

"I'm not, Rick," Josh said, walking out from behind his desk. "Ms. Flanagan was just leaving."

"Okay. Let me know when you want to go over the Op-Com contract," Rick said with a last grin as he left.

"Good-bye, Katie," Josh said as he came around his desk.

"We still have a few things to settle," Katie said in protest as he fastened his hand to her elbow, turning her toward the door.

"No, we don't." His voice was implacable.

"You'd better think the situation over carefully," Katie advised angrily as he moved her toward the door. "Don't make me get ugly about this!"

With this magnificent, though vague utterance, she shook off his hand and stalked from the office.

"Is your visitor babe gone?" Rick asked fifteen minutes later as he sauntered back into Josh's office.

"She's gone." Josh didn't comment on his friend's description of Katie. Remembering her lithe body and long, long legs, he couldn't disagree with Rick's designation of her appeal. The last two years had turned Katie's girlish assets into something definitely more womanly. He'd have had to be dead not to notice, but he also knew better than to let Katie Flanagan's sexual lure infect his brain.

His worst misjudgment—Erin Flanagan—hadn't had a fifth of her younger sister's current potency. He'd realized after Erin left him that her defection had enraged more than hurt him. He'd been seduced by the thought of belonging to a family again. But there was no way he'd let an even more lethal Katie get her hooks in him now. He thought of that frothy, curly red hair and those long, long legs and her curves ripened to the point of perfection. She'd definitely grown up since he had seen her last.

Erin had always said their family grew late bloomers, but who'd've thought Katie would blossom like this? All that feminine allure combined with her sassy exuberance left him feeling like he needed sunglasses just to look at her.

But he had too much at stake right now to get distracted. This next promotion would set the seal on his career direction.

Only a moron ignored the reality that success equaled money and money meant security. No fool, he'd figured that out at the tender age of nine when his parents had died, leaving him and his brother destitute. After his brief insanity in offering to legitimize Erin's baby and then being jilted by her, he'd realized what he really needed was financial security. Family could come later.

"So did you find your redhead in the phone book under Escorts?" Rick asked with a leer as he sank into the same chair Katie had recently vacated.

"Of course not," Josh said, annoyed. The past two years may have added a vivid, erotic sheen to Katie's cheerful sexiness, but, Flanagan though she was, the girl he remembered wouldn't sink to being an "escort."

"Kidding," Rick said, immediately inserting a placating

note in his voice in response to the frown on Josh's face. "We're not on a high enough level yet to be able to get away with trysting in the office."

"No, we're not." Josh pulled the Op-Com contract out of a file. "Katie Flanagan's just part of a business deal I'm getting rid of."

"I can't imagine why you'd want to get rid of her, but never mind. Speaking of business," Rick went on, "handling this contract to the company's advantage can only help your bid for Moore's job when he retires."

"I know." Josh looked across the desk at his friend, his jaw tightening. "I'm determined to get that promotion."

"More power to you," Rick said. "If I'd been here as long as you, I'd give you a race for your money. Playing with the big boys, earning the big money. Hell, who cares if you have to give up a personal life?"

"Anything worth having involves trade-offs," Josh said. He knew better than anyone what stability meant. What was the use of having a family if you couldn't provide for them, couldn't make sure they would be taken care of if something happened to you?

A personal life could wait.

Lowering his voice, Rick glanced over his shoulder at the nearly closed office door. "Of course, once you get to that level, you don't have to buy escorts' attentions. You can afford your own trophy wife like Williams."

Josh agreed with a contemptuous smile. "Williams is so unoriginal, he actually bought a Porsche the same week he divorced his first wife."

"I'm telling you," Rick said, "it's the corporate game. Play it or lose. Williams's young new wife gives him points with the other guys. Kind of a law of the jungle thing. Hard work will only get you so far. You ought to get yourself a trophy babe."

"I don't have a wife to divorce," Josh protested with a laugh.

"Even better," his friend said, grinning. "Allows you to accessorize more quickly. You know, find a woman who looks like your recent visitor and mount her on your wall. All the vice presidents have younger wives who spend their days getting their nails done and picking up their husbands' laundry."

"If I *mount* her, it won't be on the wall." Josh shook his head, amused by his friend's on-target depiction of life at the top. "I also don't have time for a family."

"Oh, we're not talking about a family; just a trophy wife. That kind of relationship frees up your time, from what I can tell," Rick said, mockery in his tone. "Kind of like having an artificially enhanced secretary who never complains how late you work or how many vacations get canceled. Plus you get to sleep with her."

An image popped into Josh's mind. Katie's slender body with her delectable, nonenhanced breasts pouting prettily under her snug sweater. With her glowing skin and her bright red-gold hair, she drew the eye like the heated flame of maple leaves in the fall.

The woman was definitely trophy material. At least, she would have been if she had a steady, reliable bone in her body.

Josh wrenched his thoughts away from Katie Flanagan, returning to the goal that haunted his nights and drove his days. "I can do the job and I'd like to get the promotion on my own merits, thank you."

"Yeah, that's a nice idea," Rick said with faint mockery, "but get real. Remember Sanders?"

Josh frowned. "Yes."

"He was stuck here rubber-stamping old deals for three years . . . until his wife found out he was doing the dirty with that coed."

"I remember."

"Some people around here thought the mess of the divorce would be the end of his career," Rick recalled cheerfully. "But it wasn't two months after his wife left him and he moved in with his honey that he got promoted to the London office."

"Yes." Josh had never liked Sanders much. The guy slacked off too much.

"Play the game the way the big boys do. That's my motto," Rick declared. "Give me another year and I'll be scouting for a bimbo of my own."

Everything about the idea left a bad taste in Josh's mouth. He'd never been a particularly sensitive guy, but establishing a personal relationship solely for the purposes of his career smacked of deceit. It jarred his sense of fair play to trick a woman that way.

"You need to get yourself a very visible chickie baby," his friend recommended.

Josh couldn't see himself doing it. It was the habit of a lifetime to make only promises he meant to keep.

"I want this promotion." His words were abrupt.

"Yep," Rick agreed. "Blind ambition is big-time under-rated. You have a real opportunity here with Moore's imminent retirement. They have to decide soon on who to move into his position."

"I know." Josh flipped through the contract.

"So," Rick said, "you have to make your move right away. You're not the only one who wants that spot and you've got two or three others with more seniority."

"Tough," Josh said, not looking up. "I want that job and I'll bust my butt to get it."

"Williams is your ticket," his friend declared. "You've saved his skin too many times to count."

"And now it's time to collect on that debt," Josh said. Going after this promotion was a big move, he knew, and, if he hoped to sell the big boys on his potential, he couldn't afford any distractions.

Katie's delectable image flitted into his mind. She'd come here with her brilliant smile and lush body expressly for the purpose of getting his leniency on the foreclosure.

He didn't even try to deny the drum roll of attention she'd drawn from his body. But no matter how succulent she looked, he had one focus and nothing to spare for anything or anyone that didn't further his goal.

Katie placed a bucket under another drip and swore silently at the steady drumming of rain on the roof. The *plinks* and *plonks* of a dozen different leaks seemed to mock her. Grandpa's studio needed a roof in the worst way. Priority number one.

Just as soon as Josh came to his senses about the loan.

She felt bad about the way their meeting had gone. His anger with her sister was understandable. After all, the situation hadn't been pretty. Most men would have had hard feelings about being dumped that way, even more so if they'd proposed marriage just to help the woman out. Still, it had been two years ago, and Josh really didn't have a right to hold it against her, no matter how many times she'd been engaged.

Picking her way through the maze of pots and pans on the floor, Katie tried to ignore the studio's general disarray. No wonder Erin had run off. She'd probably figured it was easier than organizing fifty years of Granddaddy's professional litter.

Yet the place held memories for Katie—the faint smell of chemicals Granddaddy used for developing photographs; the dusty collection of feather boas in the storage room. The walls in the hallway and reception area were hung with pictures from a glamorous era long gone. Beauties with penciled brows and full red lips, frozen in a flash of youth.

Even in Katie's young days, her grandfather's business had been waning, but never had that reality affected his time with her. He'd greeted her as if she were his own princess, inviting her to play with his ancient collection of cameras while he coaxed one more smile out of elderly ladies long past their bloom.

Her determination to resurrect the studio had as much to do with Granddaddy as it had to do with her own need for a place for herself. She'd taken a number of wrong turns careerwise. But somehow, she just knew this was it. Here she'd find herself surrounded by grandfather's spirit and somehow manage to prove herself, at last.

She'd just have to hope that Josh would be reasonable and not call her impulsive bluff. Heck, the radio call-in show probably didn't exist anymore and, if it did, who'd care about Josh's actions now?

She hadn't meant to threaten him, but her brush-fire

temper had gotten the better of her and the words tripped out of her mouth before she knew it.

Things like that happened all too often to her, Katie reflected mournfully, setting a pot under yet another drip.

A bell jingled as the heavy glass door swung shut behind Josh. Removing his lightweight trench coat with disgust, he shook rain droplets from his hair.

He glanced around at the dismal reception area. The place was a mess. Josh glared at the peeling wallpaper, a faded pink background for an array of glamour portraits from the fifties. The rug beneath his feet, probably once pink like the walls, now looked an odd shade of gray.

A drop of water landed on his shoe. Josh looked balefully at his Johnston and Murphy shoes, the carpet sodden beneath his foot.

How appropriate. Unquestionably, Katie Flanagan was aiming to be his own little storm cloud.

When she'd bounced into his office the day before, he'd been momentarily stunned. Most men would have taken pause if a tall, sexy redhead had sailed into their offices in a skirt short enough to stop traffic: a tall, sexy, curvaceous redhead.

From the first time he'd met her, she'd been impulsive and passionate in everything she did. She had been maddeningly argumentative, picking fights just to get under his skin. Unfortunately, she still had the power to rile him.

His immediate surge of lust the day before had been followed by an overwhelming urge to throttle her. On sight. Even before she'd opened her mouth and so artlessly demanded he extend the loan.

Katie had always brought out the beast in him. He used to tell himself that it had only been his inexperience at the time, that she wouldn't be able to get a rise out of him now. He was supposed to have matured past the urge to paddle her behind with his bare hand.

Wrong. The only difference in his response to her now was the urge to do more than spank her shapely derrière.

Crossing the studio's reception area, Josh thought about his upcoming promotion. Success equaled stability and control. He was determined to have both, and this promotion was the answer. No one had ever been considered for vice president at the tender age of twenty-nine, but, by God, he was going to make it, Flanagans or no Flanagans.

Katie's idiotic threat about calling the radio show left him cold. After Erin had betrayed and embarrassed him, what more could Katie do to make the situation worse?

Josh pushed through the velveteen curtain that led to the studio. Since the front door had been unlocked, someone must be here. Unless Katie had failed to lock up.

He walked down a hall and into a large studio. There, she stood poised like a ballerina in the center of a large room, a pan in one outstretched hand as she reached to catch a leak.

She wore some sort of colorful tights that swept lovingly over the graceful length of her legs—legs that went on and on, surmounted by that shapely fanny.

To distract himself from the lush possibilities of her body, Josh looked around the room. Walls that must have once been black were now a rusty brown, a torn backdrop drooped against the far wall. Clutter filled every corner.

An expanse of room stretched between him and the spot where Katie teetered on one foot, thrusting her pot onto an unidentifiable pile that hunkered in a shadowed corner. The open area looked like a minefield of kitchenware, and the sound of dripping water relentless.

"So I guess you're going for a kind of rain forest look?" he ventured, enjoying the startled look on Katie's face as she turned.

"Good grief," she straightened irritably, "don't you knock?"

"You didn't hear me tapping on the curtain?" He strolled across the room, sidestepping to avoid a Dutch oven.

"No," Katie replied, clearly unnerved.

Josh smiled. She felt at a disadvantage, unsure of what to expect. Good. He'd planned it that way.

"Hand me that bucket," she told him, pulling a ladder away from the wall.

He snagged the bucket and extended it to her as she climbed up the ladder, stretching to place the container on an air duct near the ceiling.

Josh saw the ladder sway and reached out automatically, his hand wrapping around her calf. Katie gasped and looked down at him as the ladder steadied beneath her.

Through the thin tights, her leg was firm and warm. Josh looked at his hand, still holding her.

Okay, so he wanted to have sex with Katie Flanagan.

Not a big deal. Most men probably developed lust at just the sight of her, much less the feel of her firm, silky leg. He wondered for a moment what would happen if he just slid his hand up a little. . . .

"Thanks," Katie said, her voice strangled. "It's steady now."

"What?"

"The ladder," she said. "It's steady now."

"Of course." Josh removed his hand, despite the urgings of his baser self.

"I'm glad you came by," she said once she was off the ladder. "Can't you see what great potential this place has? Particularly once we get the roof fixed."

Josh laughed. He couldn't help himself, despite the fact that his libido was negotiating with him on how he could tell her off while still keeping open the possibility of sex between them.

"I know it looks pretty shabby," Katie said, her voice defensive. "But it's mostly just cleanup."

He looked around derisively.

"Come here," she said suddenly, taking him by the arm. "Let me show you everything. We have three studios. This is the largest. There are dressing rooms down the end of the hall."

Her touch on his arm sent a surge through Josh, although he knew she was selling him hard on an idea that had no hope. Certainly not if it depended on his continued financial backing. He was having no further involvement with any Flanagan.

"We have two storage rooms filled with costumes and props," she continued eagerly, "and my Granddaddy's darkroom is over here. It's got all this great equipment."

She whipped open a door, above which hung a dusty red lightbulb.

"I've seen it before . . ." he started as she urged him into the small room.

"Just check it out," Katie insisted, shutting the door behind them and switching on a weird light as a strange chemical smell invaded Josh's nose.

The closetlike space held several cabinets containing trays of long-dried solutions for developing photographs. A wire Josh assumed was for hanging drying photos ran across one side of the room and some sort of ancient equipment was mounted on the far wall.

"Isn't this great?" she asked, sounding breathless again.

Josh turned, feeling her close behind him, his body reacting to her nearness with enough heat to create steam from his rain-spotted clothes. If he leaned forward slightly, he could catch a whiff of her perfume, a subtle scent of woman and flowers. It was insanity to think he could actually smell it amidst the chemical residue in the darkroom, but she was that near. He could reach out and stroke her bare arm without even moving.

Josh felt himself hardening.

"Is Erin in on this studio thing with you?" he asked abruptly, needing something to break the mental paralysis her proximity brought.

"No," she said, moving to open the door. "She's got her own things going, but she's given me her blessing."

"How kind of her," he said sarcastically.

"Anyway," Katie said, moving back into the main studio, "there's a lot of potential here. The location is good and we have the studio's reputation to build on."

"Don't start saying 'we,' " Josh objected, knowing he had to stop her before her hopes rose too high. "I only came by today to tell you to find another patsy."

"Patsy!" she gasped.

"Yes." He sauntered toward the middle of the room. "I know I told you so when you came to my office, but I remember a few things about you. And one of them is that you tend to hear what you want to hear. So I'm saying it again. I'm not extending the note."

"Be reasonable," she pleaded, looking up at him appealingly.

"Save the charm," he recommended. "I'm not caving."

She'd been an annoying, irritating pain when he was briefly engaged to her sister and he wasn't letting her twist his arm on this deal. It was time to clean this one error in judgment off his record.

Staring at him in disgust, Katie felt her temper start to boil. Amazing! With a few words, Josh had driven out any sympathy she might have had for him because of Erin's behavior and replaced it with wrath. The man had a knack for making her nuts.

Of course, he'd started some serious heat in her when he'd grabbed her leg and when they'd been crammed into the darkroom, but she didn't want to think about that. He'd just been saving her from crashing to the floor when he steadied her, for heaven's sake, not making a pass.

Not only that, he was her sister's ex-fiancé, even if they hadn't really been in love.

She had to get beyond this physical awareness thing. He wasn't even all that likable now that he'd grown into a hard, cold businessman. Which was way too bad, from her point of view, because as good-looking as he was, he could start a fire in the pit of a woman's stomach at fifty paces.

Katie glared at him. "I'm not giving up, Josh. You'd better reconsider."

"I'm not changing my mind," Josh said coolly. "So you'd better move on to yet another career option because I'm through with Flanagan insanity."

Two

"Hello! Anyone here?" A voice called out from the reception area.

Katie and Josh both turned just as a short blond young woman walked through the curtained doorway.

"Bethany!" Katie said, welcoming her friend with a smile. "Did you find the place without any trouble?"

"Yes. You give terrific directions." Bethany glanced around at the decayed, damp studio before pronouncing, "This place is a wreck."

From across the room, Josh cleared his throat, his blue eyes reflecting a grim satisfaction. "I couldn't agree more. I'm going now, Katie, but remember what I said and listen to your friend. She, at least, seems to have some sense."

"Thanks," Bethany murmured, eyeing him with polite interest. "Don't run off on my account."

But Josh had already disappeared through the curtain and seconds later the bell on the door jangled his departure.

"Who was that rather attractive thundercloud?" Bethany asked, her brows raised.

Katie giggled. "He certainly looked thunderous, didn't he?"

"Decidedly," Bethany said, adjusting a pot under a drip in her usual efficient manner.

"I don't know what I'm going to do about him," Katie said, sighing as she watched another leak appearing on the ceiling. "Unfortunately, Josh holds a mean grudge. And he's my only hope of restoring this place."

"Oh!" Realization dawned on Bethany's face. "The old boyfriend."

"He was never my boyfriend," Katie corrected her crossly. "And he was only going to marry Erin because she was pregnant. And not with his child."

"Whatever," Bethany shrugged, looking around the room again. "Are you really going to try and get this place going again?"

Katie's frown cleared. "Yes. I love it. My whole history is here. I learned how to do portraiture work with my grandfather and I know I can make a go of this place. Maybe do some boudoir work as a sideline."

"That should be interesting," her friend commented dryly. "Middle-aged women trying to put some fire back into their marriages with artfully draped chiffon and kind lighting?"

"It's more than that," Katie disagreed. "Men are stimulated visually and some women would rather be that stimulus than have their husbands sneaking peaks at lingerie catalogs."

"I suppose," Bethany said, shrugging. "Not being married or otherwise involved for any length of time, I have no real experience with the care and feeding of the average male."

"Me, neither," Katie admitted. "At least, no long-term

experience. Of course, none of this may matter. If I can't get Josh to extend the loan, the studio's washed up."

Bethany looked at the curtained doorway. "But he was here. I've been trying to get clear of my exams to call and ask. Didn't the meeting go well the other day?"

"No, it went terribly." Katie nudged a pot with her foot.

"Then why was he here?" her friend inquired logically.

Katie looked at her glumly, not eager to admit to her impulsive threat. "To answer something I said, but don't ask me what. I don't want to talk about it."

"Oh, a secret," Bethany said. "Come on, tell Auntie Beth. I swear it won't leave this room."

"It's not a secret," Katie evaded. "At least, not exactly. Things just . . . didn't go as I'd planned."

"They never do," Bethany observed with a knowledge-able air. "You're incredibly, idiotically optimistic."

"Thanks." Katie slumped onto a stained satin slipper chair. How could Josh be so cold and uncaring? He'd always been a no-nonsense type, which always brought out the worst in her, but he'd never been so hard before.

"So what happened at this meeting?" Bethany perched on a stool next to Katie, her expression genuinely sympathetic.

"Josh was very . . . unfriendly, and I lost my temper," Katie admitted. "And I said some things I shouldn't have said."

"Like . . . ?" Her friend coaxed.

"Well, he laughed at me when I asked him a tiny favor—"

"Extending a defaulted loan isn't a tiny favor," Bethany reminded her, her voice dry.

"No, but it's not like he's missing the money or that

he'll get much out of foreclosing on the studio in its current condition. It's in his best interest to give me some time to pull the place together."

"And when he laughed at you," Bethany prompted again, "you did a silly girly thing like slap him?"

"No!" Katie straightened up in indignation. "I just mentioned the radio call-in show, and . . . said I'd call in and tell them he's foreclosing on me out of spite."

"And this worried him?" Bethany asked skeptically.

"No." Katie frowned. It had been a silly threat, but once the words were out of her mouth, she hadn't known how to take them back. And Josh had made her so mad she'd forgotten everything else in her haste to *show* him.

"The man who just left here didn't look like he was shaking in his boots," her friend said dispassionately.

"No. Apparently he doesn't care one way or the other if I meant to call that radio show. Josh just came by to tell me he wasn't reconsidering his position on the loan," Katie finished glumly.

"Men!" Bethany said in feigned disgust.

"I just don't know what to do," Katie sighed. "Half the time he makes me crazy and the other half, I just want to . . ."

"Get naked with him?" Bethany supplied.

"No!" Katie denied quickly. "He makes me want to strangle him."

"Covert lust." Bethany's eyes twinkled with mischief. "Find lust wherever you can get it, I always say."

"No, you don't!" Katie retorted, veering away from her friend's observant comment. "You don't even go out on dates."

"The only men who ask me out are losers," Bethany

said, repeating an argument they'd been over before. "So what are you going to do about your problem with Josh?"

"Suicide by chocolate sounds good. Running away to Tahiti. Dying my hair blond and trying out for *Baywatch*."

"Nah. There's gotta be another way. I hear hair color is hell on redheads."

"There isn't any other way to get the studio going again. I'm doomed to be a failure at everything I try."

Bethany stared into space. "If he won't deal, it looks like you're beat."

"No, I'm not," Katie declared stubbornly, her despondency lifting. "I can't give up! One way or the other, I'll make Josh give me another chance. He's got to extend that note. I won't accept failure this time."

Katie slammed the van's cargo door shut with relief. She was determined to get Josh's attention and prove her seriousness about this profession, all at once.

Talking the dog show promoter into letting her take publicity shots had been a breeze compared to loading the dogs into the van. Who knew that a mid-sized pug could weigh so much?

Fortunately, the German shepherd was a cooperative animal since they'd had to load his carrier in the van first and then coax the dog into it.

"Here, Davinia," Katie said to her model as she hoisted the last pet carrier. "You hold Geraldo on your lap."

"Okay," the girl said, eyeing the orange tabby cat in the carrier with uncertainty.

Dressed in a toga that looked like something created

out of her mother's sheets, Davinia disappeared around the van, the protesting cat in her hands.

Hustling around to the driver's side, Katie climbed into the borrowed van with a prayer of thanks for Bethany's brother who ran a yard care business. It was pure luck to have a friend who had a van he was willing to loan.

Shifting the engine into drive, Katie eased the van out of the driveway, mindful of her noisy cargo.

The drive to Josh's building took only a few minutes. On the way, Katie replayed her conversation with the dog show promoter. Well, it wasn't actually a conversation. She'd begged and groveled for the job and the promoter had probably caved in out of sheer embarrassment.

It wasn't much, but it was a photography job.

The pet carriers in the back of the van contained one genial shepherd, the zaftig pug and a yippy, menacing Chihuahua. The dog show lady had insisted on the Chihuahua.

Now, Geraldo had been her own idea. In her mind's eye, she could see a shot of three dogs eyeing a yellow pussy cat. It worked visually.

That photography award in high school hadn't been a fluke. She could do this job and she'd prove it to Josh Morgan if she died trying.

The idea to use the plaza and fountain in front of his office building as a backdrop for her photographic efforts came to her in a flash. It would kill two birds with one stone: Why not make money while demonstrating her devotion to her craft? Supercilious, too-sexy-for-his-own-good Josh would have undeniable proof of her intentions when he got a load of this morning's endeavors.

"How's Geraldo holding up?" Katie asked Davinia, becoming conscious of low growls from the seat next to her, despite the various moans, barks and yips from the back.

The girl lifted the cat carrier to peer inside. "I don't think he likes small spaces."

Geraldo let out a yowl to punctuate her understatement.

"Well, we're almost there," Katie said. "We'll let him out as soon as we can."

Davinia lowered the cat carrier onto her lap again and stared ahead with an almost vacant complacency.

Katie shot the girl a glance. She hadn't originally envisioned needing a model for this shoot, but Davinia's mother, the dog show promoter, had other ideas. And since Katie had begged for the job, it seemed silly to quibble over giving Davinia a career boost.

If the pale, listless teenager had modeling aspirations, good for her.

Minutes later, Katie swung the van into the parking lot nearest to the front of Josh's building. Unloading the equipment was her first priority. The increasing animal noises from the rear of the van spurred her on.

She glanced at her watch, estimating how long it would take to set up the lights, camera and reflectors. Hopefully Josh wouldn't go to lunch before noon.

There was time. She'd set up the equipment and be busily employed and looking industrious by the time he came out of the building.

If he came by. Katie glanced up at the building. It would just be her luck for the man to work through the noon meal.

Regardless, she remembered that his office looked out over the plaza. Even if he was too absorbed to glance down at the plaza, someone in his office would see her and spread the word.

Katie had worked in several offices, doing temp jobs. She'd learned how efficient the grapevine could be.

One way or the other, Josh had to notice her.

The fountain situated in front of his office building was an impressive piece. A wide shallow basin caught the spray that fell from six different jets. In the middle, graceful maidens frolicked with several dog statues at their feet.

Katie supposed they could have been wolves, but the dog metaphor still worked. Pure karma. She'd have shot the photos in front of the fountain regardless, just in the hope of impressing Josh, but the dog thing sealed it.

With Davinia's help, she unloaded everything and scurried around setting up the tripod and lights. Eyeing the fountain for the best angle, Katie positioned the lights from instinct. Fortunately the weather was perfect— slightly overcast with no midday glare from the sun.

The occasional passerby gawked politely, reassuring Katie that a photo shoot was unusual enough to draw attention. She'd even remembered to ask the building leasing office for permission to use the plaza. The last thing she needed was to be hauled off to jail for misusing private property.

Unable to keep herself from glancing over her shoulder at Josh's building, Katie hurried to finish the setup, very aware of the increasing howls from the back of the van. The natives were restless.

Davinia stood to the side as Katie made the last few adjustments, the girl's fluttery toga catching the occasional breeze.

"Okay, let's unload the dogs." Katie opened the van

door, a chorus of woofs and howls greeting her. "Okay, boys. Calm down. We don't want you getting worked up before the big moment."

One by one they got the dogs out, leashing them immediately. Davinia held the panting shepherd's lead while Katie hauled the pug out.

The Chihuahua was last. Katie eased him out carefully, trying to avoid his sharp little teeth, which he showed frequently with a bulge-eyed, disagreeable growl, nothing like the cute Chihuahua on those television commercials.

"Yes, Little Joe," Katie crooned, longing to snarl back at the dog. "We're getting you out of that nasty carrier."

The dog growled again.

When the canine models were all leashed, they let Geraldo out of his cage to roam the van. Getting a whiff of the previous dog occupants, Geraldo's tail puffed out and he hissed at the empty carriers.

Leaving the cat to fight shadows in peace, Katie walked Davinia to her spot right in front of the fountain. For the best shot, she needed the girl to stand immediately next to the bowl, despite the fact that the occasional breeze blew a scatter of spray over her.

"Now, Davinia, you're the patron goddess of dogs," Katie improvised, vaguely aware that models were supposed to be acting out a part of some kind. "You're out for a stroll with your beloved pooches. You're very regal and everything."

"Okay," Davinia agreed, not looking at the dogs, which were sniffing around. The German shepherd hiked its leg on the side of the fountain.

Actually, that might have been a good shot if Katie had been doing a shoot for an artsy clothing ad campaign. But since she was doing publicity stills for a dog show, Katie let the moment pass, stepping back to check the camera's exposure and aperture.

Through the lens, she could see Davinia staring off vacantly into space, the dogs' leashes drooping from her hand as her toga slipped off one pale, thin shoulder.

At her feet, the Chihuahua snapped at the pug, who'd apparently wandered into Little Joe's territory.

Katie couldn't resist a glance at Josh's building. She was ready. If he came out now, he'd have to get a load of the totally professional setup she'd managed.

Loud barking brought her attention back to the tableau before the fountain. She stepped behind the camera and captured several shots. "Okay, Davinia. Change your position."

Davinia looked at her blankly.

"Turn the other way, lift your arm, just anything that'll look good," Katie directed her haphazardly.

The girl turned to look toward the building, her body a mirror reflection of the earlier pose.

Katie sighed. Davinia wasn't the liveliest model to work with. "Look down at the dogs."

Davinia looked down.

From the van behind Katie, loud meowing could be heard. She glanced over her shoulder and saw Geraldo, paws propped on the window as he yowled through the crack at the top.

Turning back, Katie squeezed off a few more shots, trying to direct some life into Davinia's goddess portrayal. The dogs seemed calm enough. Only the Chihuahua continued to grumble irritably at the pug, nipping at its tail. The pug growled in return. Above them, the German shepherd smiled good-naturedly. Actually, it seemed to have a lot in common with Davinia, in terms of temperament.

Katie captured a few more angles, shifting to catch the fountain spray in the frame.

"That looks good, Davinia," she called. "Wait there for a minute and I'll get Geraldo."

Now that he was free of his pet carrier, Geraldo seemed much more cheerful. He greeted Katie with the loud rumble of a purr, positioning his orange-striped body to rub against her hand.

"Good kitty," Katie rewarded him. "Come and let Davinia hold you for a few minutes. Don't you worry about those doggies. They're not going to bother you."

The possibilities of sparking a canine uproar occurred to her, but the dog show promoter assured Katie that her dogs were too civilized to chase cats.

Katie was crossing her fingers on that promise.

"Here." She plopped Geraldo into Davinia's arms.

The girl looked down at the cat in surprise, her thin eyebrows raised.

"Just hold him," Katie instructed her. "Keep the dogs' leashes in one hand and hold Geraldo up high on your chest. I'll take a few shots and we'll be done."

"Okay," Davinia replied with faint interest.

Katie stepped back behind the camera, her attention totally focused on the scene before her. Through the lens she saw Davinia in her fluttering toga clutching Geraldo to her chest, the leashes threaded through her slender hand. The shepherd sat on his haunches panting happily while Little Joe took another nip at the pug, which prompted a more menacing growl from his victim.

Using both the camera on the tripod and another in her

hand, Katie shifted to get the best angles, snapping off a string of shots.

"What the hell are you doing here?"

Josh's irritated voice startled her. Katie swung around to see him, her surprise giving away to pure satisfaction.

He stood next to her, looking like power incarnate in his eight-hundred-dollar business suit, his beautiful blue eyes blazing with suspicion.

"I'm working," she said perkily. Behind her, the sound of growling grew louder.

"Why here?" he asked, his jaw tight as his gaze flashed over her face.

"Oh, I have permission to shoot around the fountain, Katie responded airily, trying to ignore the tango rhythm her heart had picked up with his presence.

"Permission?"

"Yes, that's how we professionals do it." The sound of Little Joe's resounding growls drew her attention back to Davinia, waiting placidly beside the fountain.

"Now, if you'll excuse me for a moment," said Katie smugly, "I need to finish this. I'll be right with you."

"If you'll excuse me?" Josh repeated, clasping her arm, his tone low and angry. "What I have to say won't take a minute."

Katie turned back to him, keeping half an eye on the pug and Chihuahua, who were now circling each other in front of Davinia.

"I'm glad you're working. If you keep at it, you won't need to harass people to get financing. Develop some skills and a track record and some bank will give you a loan on merit." His tone did more than border on condescending.

She stiffened, a surge of pure anger bolting through her. "Listen, you stubborn—"

A shriek from Davinia cut through Katie's retort.

"Help!" the girl cried. The pug was chasing the Chihuahua, and they were wreathing their leashes around her like ribbons on a maypole. "Help!"

By this time the shepherd had cheerfully entered the fray, chasing the pug, who in turn appeared to be chasing Little Joe.

"Stop!" Katie cried, setting her camera down as a hissing Geraldo began to ascend Davinia's body, drawing more shrieks from the girl.

With an exclamation of disgust, Josh strode forward, attempting to catch the Chihuahua by its collar. Within seconds, a churning mass of dogs had managed to upend a light, which fell with a crash just short of the fountain.

Katie breathed a quick sigh of relief that they'd avoided electrifying the water in the fountain. The situation was turning into enough of a debacle without her light shorting out the entire block.

"Help, help, help," wailed Davinia as the dog fight continued around her. She teetered, her legs bound together by the leashes.

Josh reached out to catch her, wading into the seething, snapping cluster of dog fur.

He stretched his arm out just as the shepherd jumped up, and canine forelegs hit him square in the back.

"Ooof!"

Josh was off balance with no place to regain his footing amid snarling dogs, and he fell forward.

Davinia, with Geraldo now atop her head, shrieked as

Josh fell against her. The low edge of the basin surrounding the fountain caught her right behind the knees.

Katie covered her eyes, peeking through just in time to see the impact. With a *sploosh*, they hit the water, sending up a shower of droplets.

Josh, Geraldo, Davinia and the Chihuahua went under en masse. The pug landed on the edge of the fountain, a smile on his broad face.

Unable to bear the sight, Katie closed her eyes tight and covered her ears. She figured they had to surface and Josh would do so with her name on his lips.

A few seconds later, she opened her eyes to the sound of splashing water and muttered swearing.

"Flanagan, get over here!" Josh ordered. "Yeeoow!"

Katie grimaced as a desperate Geraldo, claws extended, climbed Josh's leg.

"Here, kitty, kitty." She leaned forward and carefully plucked the panicked cat from his pants.

"You," Josh said with loathing, "are an accident looking for a victim."

"I'm sorry." Katie struggled to find the words to reclaim the situation even though she knew it was hopeless.

He bent to disentangle Davinia from the dog leashes and rescue Little Joe, who was treading water nearby.

"Look, Josh," she said, regaining her equilibrium. "This could have happened to just anybody."

Sparing her a fulminating glance, Josh climbed out of the fountain. "But things like this *usually* happen to you."

As he sloshed by her, his beautifully cut suit coat slapping with every step, he paused. "Stay away from me, Katie Flanagan. Far, far away."

* * *

Juggling the Klemper file in one hand and a stack of letters in the other, Josh walked out of his office. As usual, he was up to his ears in decisions that should have been made yesterday, possibly the day before.

"Ms. Harper"—he stopped beside his secretary's desk, still perusing his notes—"I need you to find—"

"I'm sorry, Mr. Morgan," she interrupted, her voice anxious, "but this young woman would like to see you. She doesn't have an appointment."

Noticing for the first time the presence of someone standing in front of Sara Harper's desk, Josh looked up.

Katie.

It had been a week since his disastrous dip in the fountain. A short, pleasant, Flanagan-free week.

Wearing a form-fitting suit of some silky off-white material with a skirt that revealed miles of leg, Katie looked like an invitation to Fantasyland.

"Hi, Josh." Her blue eyes challenged him as she leaned forward slightly, gracefully poised against his secretary's desk. "Do you have a few minutes to talk?"

Her movement accentuated the soft mounds of her breasts, which were rising and falling ever so slightly with her breath. Exercising extreme discipline, Josh tore his gaze away from the hint of cleavage displayed by the cut of her suit.

"I'm very busy," he said, keeping his eyes trained on her face while trying not to be distracted by the curve of her satin lips. "And as long as you're not drowning anybody in the fountain out front, we don't have anything to talk about. Good-bye, Katie."

"Josh!" She straightened indignantly. "That wasn't completely my fault and I only need a few minutes of your time."

"No," he said, his vulnerability to her sex appeal making his voice harder than he'd intended. If he went with his inclinations, he'd offer her a quick fifteen minutes on the top of his desk. She could talk all she wanted.

"You're not being fair," Katie said, her voice dropping slightly as she shifted toward him.

The shimmer of that suit over her curves just about undid him. One slight shift and all sorts of ripples spread through his body. No doubt about it, he was in major lust mode.

The only thing to do was to shut her out. Focus on the mountain of things to be done. Work, work, work. Be proactive and keep focusing on the promotion.

Any contact with Katie threatened his focus, and he'd worked too hard to get distracted now. Even the most innocent encounter with her could likely have disastrous repercussions on his mental focus.

Still exercising discipline, Josh turned away to address his secretary. "Ms. Harper, I need you to place a call to Deidra Marks. I believe you have her number on file?"

"Yes, sir." Ms. Harper nodded, grabbing a pencil and notepad.

"She's agreed to accompany me to the dinner meeting this evening with Mr. and Mrs. Williams. I'd planned on picking her up"—Josh frowned at the file in his hands—"but this Klemper situation has to be settled today. I have a meeting with Klemper late this afternoon. I'll need Ms. Marks to meet me at the restaurant."

"Yes, sir. And what restaurant is that?"

"La Prairie, at seven-thirty."

"Fine, sir. I'll call her right away."

Katie indignantly watched Josh turn toward his office. It was as if she were no longer standing there. He'd just dismissed her from his mind, brushing her off like a troublesome pest.

"Make sure Deidra knows it's important she get there on time," Josh said over his shoulder, the faintest shred of anxiety running through his words. "I need this dinner to go perfectly."

"Josh!" Katie said, frustration simmering in the one word.

"No, Katie," he shot back without pausing as he disappeared into his office.

A second later the door thudded shut behind him.

"Well, how rude!" Katie bit her lip in vexation, not sure what to do now.

"He's not usually like this," the secretary hastily assured her. "It's just that he's up for this promotion. No one's ever been offered a vice president's job so young. Mr. Morgan's just swamped, pushing himself even harder than normal. I think he even asked this Marks woman to go with him to dinner because she's very presentable."

"I see," Katie returned grimly, noting the devoted tone of the woman's words. Obviously, Josh had a fan.

So he was up for a big promotion and didn't have time to talk, Katie brooded, staring at his closed office door. The injustice of his attitude burned her.

After all, she hadn't done anything to him—well, nothing of real significance. Despite his fury toward her, she couldn't be held responsible for his falling into the fountain. But he still refused to listen to her, just because Erin had dumped him and made it known to the entire city.

The last few minutes had cleared up one thing, anyway. Josh wasn't married. Or even involved with anyone, if his secretary was to be believed. He'd invited this Deidra woman for dinner because she was "presentable."

Obviously, he didn't consider Katie presentable in any way. Josh had decided that any contact with her was detrimental, based solely on her checkered romantic history and the fact that her last name was Flanagan.

"If you'll excuse me," the secretary said, "I need to make this call for Mr. Morgan."

"Of course. Go right ahead," Katie told her, still loath to leave despite the fact that she didn't know how to get past Josh's latest roadblock.

Before coming this morning, she'd dressed carefully, in an attempt to look both attractive and presentable. Refusing to dwell on Bethany's remark about covert lust, she didn't let herself remember the breadth of Josh's shoulders and the heat that sometimes came quickly to his eyes.

Okay, so he was an attractive man. He still had the heart of a Wall Street earnings report and was stuffy to boot. Besides the fact that he was her sister's ex-fiancé, for what that was worth.

None of that mattered, however. She needed him to extend the loan—that was all.

Katie chewed on her lip. Her business experience was minimal, she knew—not really much of a reassurance when she considered what a stickler Josh had become about money.

And she would really prefer not to discuss her photography with him until the memory of their most recent debacle had faded with time.

So she was left little to work with, but she absolutely had to find a way to change his mind.

Ms. Harper was busily scrolling through her card file. Katie watched absently, her mind scrambling for options. Just how far should she go? She'd already stumbled into threatening the man with ridicule. As if her sister hadn't done enough of that.

He was such a stick-in-the-mud. Still, maybe she could make Josh's conservatism work in her favor.

"Deidra Marks," Josh's secretary mumbled to herself as she reached for the phone. "Five, five, five, seven, seven, zero, nine."

Katie found herself repeating the phone number automatically, a chant that echoed in her head. Josh was being so bullheaded, he deserved whatever he got.

"Ms. Marks?" the secretary asked. "I'm Sara Harper and I have a message for you from Mr. Morgan."

Adjusting her purse strap higher on her shoulder, Katie turned to leave the office, an idea suddenly burning in her brain.

The door closed softly behind her, shutting out the secretary's recitation of Josh's message.

Soon, very soon, Deidra Marks would be getting another message from the helpful Ms. Harper. But first Katie had to find a pencil and jot down a phone number.

Three

Josh left his Lexus with the parking attendant and made his way into the restaurant. La Prairie had earned the critics' highest ratings of culinary excellence for two decades. It also boasted the smooth, quietly expensive atmosphere to which his boss was accustomed.

Josh entered La Prairie's foyer at precisely seven-thirty, and squelched his frustration at finding it empty. He knew from past experience that while Deidra Marks was a beautiful and efficient money manager, she had a serious problem with punctuality.

Of course, there was the unlikely possibility that she'd arrived earlier and, along with Dave and Madison Williams, had been shown to their table. He could always hope.

As the maitre d' approached, Josh's thoughts buzzed with the evening ahead. For eight long years, he'd worked toward this goal. Nothing less than landing a vice presidency in a Fortune 500 company would do. And this was his chance.

Traditionally, the vice presidencies went to older men who had been with the company longer, but a few exceptions to this rule had been made in the past. Josh meant to be one of those exceptions.

When his boss had invited him to dinner, he had known what it meant. His hard work and long hours had gained him some notice. But would it be enough?

Was Rick on the right track about needing to play the game with the big boys? Although it went against his grain, to be on the safe side, Josh had arranged for a beautiful, cultured date. A woman who understood the rules and had no problem with being an accessory since she was clawing her way to the top of a similar heap.

"This way, sir," the maitre d' beckoned.

The subdued clink of cutlery and the murmur of cultured voices met Josh as he turned the corner into the main room. The sparkle of candlelight on crystal gave the scene an elegant glow.

To the far side of the linen-covered tables, a tiny dance floor separated the diners from a small band of musicians providing live music.

Josh's step quickened as he caught sight of Dave Williams's graying head across the room.

He faltered a second later when his gaze swept across the table's other occupants. To Dave's right sat his wife, a beautiful, shapely woman in her thirties, and beyond her was . . . Katie Flanagan?

Josh stared.

Maybe he was hallucinating. Had she hounded him to the brink of insanity? Or was Katie Flanagan really sitting there next to his boss?

What the hell was *she* doing here?

At that moment, Josh would have given his pension for ten minutes in a bar. Just time enough to down several straight bourbons.

No reprieve was forthcoming, however. Following the maitre d', Josh's steps brought him closer to disaster.

Katie sat at the table, a teasing smile on her luscious lips and triumph in her blue eyes. A dress of some sort of black knit material clung to her curves, baring her throat and shoulders to the gleaming candlelight. With her red-gold hair in a cloud around her shoulders and a gleam of mischief in her blue eyes, she looked like trouble incarnate.

Damn her.

Every muscle in Josh's body felt clenched. Anger rose in him, overshadowing the dismay he'd first suffered at the sight of her.

Everything he'd worked for, everything he craved was on the line tonight. His goal glimmered before him.

Katie had threatened to try and destroy him if he didn't renegotiate the loan on the studio. Was she here to make trouble with his boss? How had she found out about the promotion? About the dinner engagement tonight?

He had known better than to hope she'd just go away. Of course, she'd try and stir up as much trouble as possible. However, he hadn't expected her to be so creative about it. Or so formal.

A black-tie demolition. What the hell was she up to?

Josh forced a smile onto his face as Dave rose and extended his hand.

"Josh, boy," the older man said, a smile creasing his face. "Good to see you. You know my wife, Madison?"

"Of course," Josh said, trying to infuse a cordial note into his voice. With the anger occupying the greater part of chest, it took some doing to work in a warmer greeting.

"Good evening, Mr. Morgan. I'm so glad you and your

date could join us for dinner." Madison Williams smiled at him with genuine welcome.

"Darling," Katie stretched out a welcoming hand, "how wonderful that your meeting didn't make you late."

Well aware of the Williams's observing, Josh thrust aside his confusion and took her slender hand in his, not resisting when she pulled him down for a kiss.

It was the merest of salutes, a polite brushing of lips in a well-lit restaurant, but it left Josh feeling like a popcorn kernel in hot oil. If he'd been anywhere else, he'd have been tempted to haul her into his arms and kiss her until they both burst into flames, despite the fact that he wanted to strangle her.

He felt sexual hunger fed by rage—a wholly novel experience for him. Very few people got to him like Katie Flanagan.

The satin texture of her lips and the warm rush of her breath sent his heart rate up several notches.

He wanted to turn her over his knee and spank her before marching her out of the restaurant.

Since neither were possible at the moment, he straightened, catching a glimpse of wide-eyed breathlessness on her face as he seated himself.

Some remote part of his brain registered her response to their contact and filed it away under "puzzling." The rest of his gray matter, however, was furiously engaged in finding a way out of this predicament.

The last thing he needed was unpredictable Katie Flanagan meddling in his well-orchestrated career path. Unquestionably, if anyone could make a mess of this, it was her.

Somehow he had to neutralize her for the evening.

"Care for anything to drink before dinner?" Dave asked, beckoning to a waiter.

"No, thank you," Josh responded, knowing his wits were scrambled enough, despite his earlier urge to blunt the edges of what was shaping up to be an even trickier dinner engagement than he'd expected. The next hour or so might bring an end to his promotion hopes, but, if so, he'd face it without a blindfold.

The irony of it all almost made him laugh aloud. What man wouldn't want a date with a woman who looked like Katie? But nothing was simple here, not even lust.

How unfortunate that he couldn't have a smooth and successful dinner with her at his side. How different this evening would be if they both knew that later they'd be locked together in passion, the sweat and heat of their bodies sending them into a conflagration of ecstasy.

Mindless, simple sex. But even that would probably be foolish with Katie Flanagan.

"Had a funny thing happen on the links with Morehouse the other day," Dave Williams said, sipping his aperitif.

Josh schooled his face into attentiveness as the man launched into a golf story.

A swift sideways glance in Katie's direction showed her smiling at Josh, her eyes faintly wary.

The fountain incident and the destruction of his suit was nothing next to what she would do to him tonight, he reminded himself. Not that his boss would care about the old history with Erin, but Josh knew enough of Katie's out-of-bounds behavior to suspect she could find a hundred creative ways to embarrass both himself and his boss.

Nothing could be designed to more effectively turn his boss against him than some sort of public embarrassment.

The waiter's approach with menus interrupted Dave's story and drew Josh's attention back to the moment.

Under the cover of the Williams's discussion of their menu choices, Josh took the opportunity to lean toward Katie and murmur, "So, will Deidra Marks be arriving at any moment?"

"No," Katie murmured back, not looking up from her menu. "She understands that the dinner was canceled due to a business crisis."

Josh leaned back in his seat. "I see."

Katie had somehow gotten wind of the dinner tonight and managed to cancel his date. Josh felt his mouth thin in grim anger. He'd underestimated little Katie Flanagan. She surpassed even her sister in the scheming department.

The glance Katie flashed his way was accompanied by a pleading smile. He didn't quite understand the supplicating look, but she apparently had a game to play and he wasn't about to let her succeed.

He wouldn't allow himself to regret his refusal to reconsider the foreclosure. She'd come to him determined to cajole him into forgiving the note he held on that damned photography studio, no matter what she had to do to change his mind.

Even if her appearance in his life hadn't brought the past back with a vengeance, he still wouldn't have continued to finance her grandfather's studio.

She was unreliable. Her whole adult life had been a series of broken promises. Sooner or later, she'd get tired of the photography studio and she'd move on—having shafted him in the process.

He'd do well to remember that when she flashed him a smile with her enchanting mouth. The plan had been to simplify his life by foreclosing on the Flanagan note, not sign on for more of the same.

But here she was, complicating his life.

The waiter approached then, asking for their orders in a deferential voice.

When he'd gone, taking the expensive, embossed menus with him, Madison Williams leaned forward, her face alight. "So, Josh, Katie was telling us that the two of you have known each other for several years, but you just realized you were in love recently. How sweet to have love blossom after years of acquaintance."

Josh opened his mouth, although he didn't know what exactly would come out.

"Don't see how you could fall for this son of a gun." Dave Williams's laugh boomed out as he shadow-punched Josh. "Of course, it's obvious what he sees in you."

"Oh, Mr. Williams." Katie blushed, her smile pleased and demure. She glanced at Josh.

"It takes a real man to handle a sexy young thing," Dave boasted, puffing his chest out a little, while across the table, his wife looked down at her wineglass.

"Yes, takes a real man," Dave chuckled again.

"Mrs. Williams—" Katie began, jumping in, her words blunting the awkward silence.

"Call me Madison, please," the other woman interrupted to say, a faintly grateful expression on her face.

"Madison," Katie said, "where did you get those earrings? They're beautiful."

Watching her diversionary tactic, Josh acknowledged to himself that she'd handled an awkward moment well. Katie was surprisingly good at the social stuff. She'd been a sassy, annoying girl when he met her and the past two years had only matured her ability to give him hell. For a moment, he found himself admiring her audacity, though. Apparently, little stood between Katie and what she wanted.

Josh could understand that determination. His own goals held the same power over him. He just didn't think he'd have the guts to throw decency and honesty to the wind the way Katie did.

"You and Mr. Williams have children?"

"No." Madison Williams's smile faltered. "Dave's children are like my own. He has three from a previous marriage."

Dave Williams snorted, his smile turning even more fatuous. "She has her baby, though."

"Baby?" Katie echoed, sending a puzzled glance between the two.

"Oh, yes." Madison's face lit up. "Eden Duchesse Williams. She's a beautiful standard poodle. Purebred."

"Damn dog," Dave Williams said in an aside to Josh.

"Don't be mean." Madison fluttered her napkin at him. "You know you love her. We both do. Eden Duchesse is a champion. She takes ribbons in dog shows all the time."

"You enter her in . . . dog shows?" Katie asked, her voice a little breathless.

Josh had a sudden remembrance of dogs, water and Katie's aghast expression.

"Oh my, yes, she does well in shows. A pure-bred dog like Eden must be allowed to compete. It's vital to her temperament," Madison said earnestly.

"Dog thinks she's better than humans," Dave Williams grumbled without any real heat. "Eats out of a crystal dish, sleeps on a velvet pillow."

"Oh, Dave," Madison chastised. "You know you love her. I found the two of you taking a nap together on the couch just yesterday."

Her husband flushed. "Well, she's friendly enough."

"Is Eden Duchesse entered in the Metropolitan Area Dog Show next month?" Katie asked.

Josh wondered idly if she'd known about Mrs. Williams's dog all along. Probably not. Katie was devious enough, but he didn't see her plotting anything with such extravagant forethought. Apparently, she just lived under a watchful star that arranged serendipitous situations like this.

He, on the other hand, was reaping more than his fair share of bad luck, Flanagan-style.

"Why, yes. We've entered the Metro show for several years now," Madison answered.

Katie smiled modestly. "I did the publicity stills for the show this year."

"Really?" Madison William sounded fascinated. "You're a photographer?"

"Yes." Katie flashed Josh a defiant smile. "It's a family tradition. My granddaddy was Devin Flanagan. He had a studio on Fifth Street for almost forty years."

"Really? A photography studio?" Madison asked, interest sparkling in her eyes. "Is it the charming pink building with a curved porch and steps?"

Josh resisted the urge to sink his head into his hands. This was a nightmare. Katie had both his boss and the man's wife eating out of her hands. What was it about this woman?

"That's the place," Katie agreed, excitement on her face. "My granddaddy left the studio to me and my sister.

I'm going to fix it up and revive it to its glory days, like in the fifties."

"Oh, how wonderful," Madison breathed. "You'll be upholding a tradition. That building has such appeal. Will you be doing all the photography?"

"Yes, for now. But I may have to add several other people when business really gets going," Katie said with a typically optimistic note in her voice.

Feeling like he was about to choke on his own disgust, Josh saw with relief the waiter approaching with their meal.

When each plate had been presented with a flourish and the wine served with ritual, the waiter finally left them. Silence fell, broken only by the genteel clink of silver against china.

Josh ate mechanically, a calm sort of acceptance struggling with his urgent need to do something to avert disaster. He'd planned this meal tonight to entrench himself further with Dave Williams, sexy trophy date and all.

Firecracker Flanagan hadn't figured into his plans, however.

"Well, Josh," Dave Williams said after a moment. "I want to congratulate you on how well you've handled the Op-Com contract."

Josh said, "Thank you."

He'd been employed at the company for eight years now and he'd handled a hell of a lot more than Op-Com, maximizing his staff's performance and meeting or exceeding his sales goals, keeping under budget all the while. But now didn't seem the moment to quibble.

"I like to think of our company as nurturing young talent." Williams sat back, waving his fork in an expansive gesture. "Dedicated, trustworthy employees who know how to work hard for the company."

"Yes, sir." Josh gave up the pretense of eating, very aware of Katie beside him, and wondering at her silence.

Shouldn't she be making her move any time now? Turn and throw wine in his face. Strip naked and dance on the table?

"I was telling Morehouse the other day," Williams continued, "how fortunate we are to have you working at this level."

"Josh works harder than anyone I know," Katie put in, a smile on her lips.

He glanced at her, not letting his wariness show on his face. What the hell was she up to?

Deciding he'd go down in flames if he had to go down, Josh reached out and patted Katie's hand, winning a startled look from her. "She's such a sweetheart. So devoted . . . and reliable. Just like the rest of her family."

Katie's blue eyes seemed to cool as she absorbed his veiled insult, but the smile on her face stayed put.

"And you're . . . hard to describe," she added.

Josh saw the fire flashing in her eyes.

Okay, now *this* was it. The next words out of her mouth would send everything to hell. Whatever she was going to do or say to embarrass him, the moment had come.

Josh leaned back in his chair. All he had was bare-knuckled courage to handle having everything he'd ever wanted blow up in his face. From the time he was twelve, he'd vowed to work himself into a job that would ensure he'd never be at anyone's charity again. This job, with its security and financial compensation, would do that for him.

"Yes, yes," Dave Williams agreed. "We're all very pleased with Josh. We've got our eye on you. You've got big things ahead."

Katie sat stiffly in her chair, saying nothing.

"I appreciate your saying so, sir," Josh said slowly, unable to keep from glancing at Katie.

"Damn, this is an excellent steak," Williams said to his wife. "Have we had this here before?"

"Of course," his wife replied with the faintest asperity. "Just two weeks ago. . . ."

Unable to bear the tension, Josh leaned toward Katie.

She frowned, raising her eyebrows in question.

"You'll never have a better moment," Josh taunted her in a barely audible voice. He might have to go down in flames, but he didn't have to do it without landing a few blows of his own.

"Oh! My earring!" she said in a slightly louder than normal voice before diving her head under the tablecloth. Josh watched her in astonishment.

"Sssssst." Katie lifted the tablecloth and beckoned to him.

Glancing around self-consciously, Josh bent down.

"What did you say?" she asked him in the relative privacy afforded by the tablecloth.

Almost beyond caring that they probably looked like idiots, Josh hissed, "Why don't you just do it? Go ahead and make a scene, embarrass me in front of everyone."

"Why would I do that?" she asked in feigned astonishment, her green eyes too innocently wide.

"Get it over with," he demanded. "You said you'd do me in if I didn't help you. Just do it. Shove the knife in my back and put an end to this charade."

"Why, Josh"—she fluttered her eyelashes at him—"why would I do anything like that . . . so quickly?"

Josh heard the sound of his own swiftly indrawn breath just as the cloth on the other side of the table lifted.

Dave Williams's florid face appeared. "I guess you two lovebirds need a moment alone?"

Katie and Josh both straightened at the sound of his jovial laughter.

"I dropped my earring," Katie said, her face enchantingly flustered as she clapped a hand to her ear.

"Well, well, my dear," Williams said, his eyes positively twinkling. "Are you willing to dance now that you've found it?"

Josh almost groaned aloud.

"Why, I'd love to," declared Katie prettily. She rose, placing her slender hand on Dave Williams's arm.

Watching them weave their way through the tables, Josh almost forgot Mrs. Williams's presence at the table.

"She's such a lovely girl," Madison said in a colorless tone. "Have you two made any definite plans for the future?"

Jolted by the thought, Josh took a moment to find his tongue. "Ah, no. It really hasn't come up."

His boss's wife fetched up an empty laugh. "I bet you're one of those men who date a different girl every night. Dave says guys should play the field while they can, but they need to find a supportive wife to help build their careers."

Madison Williams sent a strained smile across the table.

"I suppose that's true," Josh replied, searching for a way to shift the conversation to a less sensitive topic. All evening he'd sensed tension between his boss and his boss's young wife. "Would you care to dance, Mrs. Williams?"

"Oh," she flushed with delight, laying her napkin aside. "I'd love to."

When they got to the dance floor, Katie and Dave Williams were already dancing, and an apparently animated conversation was taking place between them. Josh couldn't help becoming tense.

Maybe the little witch had decided to pour out her venom to Williams while they danced. What man wouldn't be inclined to listen sympathetically with a seductive armful like Katie whispering in his ear?

Would she be catty about his wife? Talk about Williams being so much older? Or maybe she'd hint that Josh was scouting around looking for a better job. Any of those tactics would bring down Williams's ire on his head.

"So Katie's a photographer," Madison Williams said, her voice impressed. "She must be very talented and very committed to her art."

Josh smiled gamely at the attractive woman, wondering how to respond to that remark. He racked his brain trying to remember if Madison Williams had a career herself or if she was more of the toenail-polishing variety of corporate wife.

Fortunately, Madison didn't seem to need much help in carrying the conversation.

"I think it's lovely that she's so devoted to reopening her grandfather's studio," the other woman said warmly. "So few people have a direction these days. I'm just sure she'll be a big success."

Only the sternest discipline kept Josh from pointing out that Katie had the barest of photographic experience, and none whatsoever at running a business. Her likelihood of success in running the studio had about the same probability as that of a snowball surviving hell.

Choosing prudence over retaliation, he merely made an assenting sound in his throat and danced Mrs. Williams toward her husband. Maybe he could overhear what they were talking about.

As they shuffled closer to the other couple, Katie's laughter rippled out.

Dave Williams's attentive face gave Josh pause. All Katie would have to do was lean closer, tell him breathlessly that she wasn't sure she should mention this, but that he really ought to know that Josh was a big meanie and wouldn't renegotiate her loan.

No, his boss wouldn't really care that Katie's hopes were blighted, but he'd care about himself being put into an awkward position. Like many small-minded men, Dave Williams was very jealous of his dignity.

If Katie embarrassed Williams, that would be the death knell for Josh's promotion. Curtains to the plans he'd first made as he worked his way through college. All because he'd wanted to clean up the leftovers from the Flanagan period of his past.

All because Katie Flanagan was a self-absorbed ditz and Williams a pompous ass.

"There you two are," Dave Williams said as their paths crossed. "Care to trade partners? I'm sure Josh can hardly wait to get Katie into his arms, and I'm always interested in groping my sexy wife in public.

"Oh, Dave," his young wife reproached him with embarrassment as she slipped from Josh's arms.

Katie waited, a wary look on her face as the other couple danced away.

From the undiminished joviality on Dave Williams's face, she hadn't said anything particularly negative about Josh.

That was strange.

Taking her hand, Josh swung Katie into the dance's rhythm, his mind busily trying to decipher his sudden realization. She hadn't said or done anything goofy all evening and he wondered now if she would.

So why the hell was she here?

Katie was quiet as they danced, the wariness still in her eyes. She felt altogether too good in his arms, her body soft and seductively close, her steps matching his with apparent ease. Josh pondered her coppery hair, sweet-smelling even at this distance.

Why had she set up this little demonstration tonight? Was she dallying with him like a cat with a mouse? Perhaps he was to be given one more chance to respond to her threats.

She'd learn he didn't bend to force.

But once again he found he had to admire her audacity. Doing so was easier now that the death of his promotion seemed less imminent.

Ever since she'd walked into his office, Josh had fought his attraction for her. She exuded life and sexuality with every breath. Yet the very ebullience and spontaneity that defined her attraction also made her a poor business risk.

What was he to do with her? With his own urge to make love to her from dusk till dawn? Sex was a simple equation, and that part of their interaction worried him less than the fact that Katie made him so angry. Made him laugh when he didn't want to. Made him forget his purpose, if even for a moment.

She was a major distraction, but could she also be an asset?

Tonight, she'd fit into his plans with perfection—better than Deidra Marks and her chilly pleasantries would have done.

The band played the closing bars of the song. Josh and Katie clapped politely with everyone else on the dance floor. But as the music started again and Katie turned to return to their table, he took her hand and pulled her back into his arms.

She looked up at him, her green eyes startled.

"I like this song," he lied with a shrug.

"So do I," she said, her face unusually solemn as he pulled her closer.

Josh had to decide what to do at this crossroads. Why had Katie come tonight, if not to embarrass him in front of his boss?

He had to find out just what she was plotting . . . and he needed to rethink Katie's role in the game at hand. Maybe they had something to offer one another after all.

Katie felt Josh's hand at the small of her back, his touch so distracting that she stumbled over her good-bye to Dave and Madison Williams.

Her sketchy plan to startle and dismay Josh hadn't evolved the way she'd hoped. Not that she'd put a whole lot of planning into it, but still, this superficially pleasant evening hadn't been what she'd envisioned. She'd thought he'd be so angry with her for usurping his date's place that he'd do anything to get rid of her.

Never had she planned on him dancing with her and humming in her ear.

Katie watched with trepidation as the other couple got into their car and drove away. Now it was just her and Josh.

Even the valet parking guy had turned away to retrieve Josh's car.

"I don't think I've mentioned how lovely you look tonight," Josh said as the parking attendant disappeared into the night.

"Thank you," she said warily, hoping her voice didn't sound as nervous as she felt.

There had been moments tonight when she could almost read Josh's thoughts when he looked at her. She'd planned on him being angry when she dreamed up her stunt for tonight. But her determination to get the money to reopen the studio sustained her. And she had to admit, she'd enjoyed tweaking him a little. Josh had grown too righteous with success.

In her hazy thinking about the evening, she'd assumed Josh would somehow get the message as to how serious she was and slip her a note agreeing to extend the loan.

She hadn't envisioned a lot of contact with him, hadn't planned on standing here on the breezy portico of the restaurant, wondering what would happen next.

Eager to escape this awkward moment, Katie fumbled for her parking ticket stub in her tiny evening purse. After finally locating it, she looked in the direction the parking attendant had taken, wondering how long he would be.

To her shock, Josh reached out and twitched the parking ticket from her hand.

"There's no need for that," he said. "I'll drive you home."

"But my car," Katie faltered, suddenly not wanting him to drive her anywhere.

"I'll have it delivered to you in the morning," Josh replied, pleasantly implacable as he pocketed the stub.

"What if I want to drive myself home?" she asked, starting to feel irritated.

He turned toward her with glinting blue eyes. "If I'm not mistaken, you want something from me."

Katie stared at him. He'd seemed startled to see her earlier in the evening, a frown hovering at the back his eyes all through dinner. But now he was calmer. Much calmer and way too in control.

"Yes, I want something from you," she admitted reluctantly. They both knew what it was.

"Then we need to talk and tonight's as good a time as any."

He sounded so reasonable, Katie almost wondered if she'd imagined his earlier ire.

"I guess so," she agreed even more reluctantly.

Just then the parking attendant drove up in a sleekly expensive sedan in a conservative silver color. Josh opened the passenger door for her, waiting as Katie got in.

As he shut her door and went around to the driver's side, she felt a moment's panic. What if he drove her to a deserted area, strangled the life out of her and dumped her body? She'd certainly provoked him. Well, maybe not to the extent of murdering her, but still, a man like Josh was used to being in charge of his fate.

He sat next to her, disturbingly attractive in his evening clothes, his hand relaxed on the wheel as he drove away from the restaurant.

The interior of the car smelled of him, a faint mixture of his aftershave and his own scent. Katie remembered that aroma from two years ago.

After giving him directions to her apartment, Katie lapsed into a chastised silence. She had no idea what he wanted to say to her, but her natural optimism began slowly to reassert itself.

Josh might be a lot of things, but he wasn't a murderer or a man prone to losing his cool. That characteristic maddened her at some level, but it was nice to rely on when she'd gone out of her way to provoke him.

They pulled up to her apartment complex, and as Katie was locating her purse, Josh again opened the car door for her. For some reason, this courtesy made her nervous, but she ignored the sensation and allowed herself to be escorted to the door.

He was coming in. She knew that because they still hadn't settled anything.

Katie unlocked the door and glanced around quickly as she entered, aware of him at her heels. She'd left her place in a rush and there was no telling what they'd find dangling from the ceiling fan.

To her surprise, the room looked fairly decent, with only a few items of clutter on the blue-green couch.

Josh closed the door behind him and stood staring around in frank appraisal. His gaze wandered over the tangle of plants by the window to her collection of art deco figurines on a far lamp table, and stopped on the huge portrait that dominated the wall above the couch. It was a closeup shot, head and shoulders, of her and her grandfather.

Taken a few years before his death, the photograph captured all the love Katie had known with him, the tenderness in his grizzled smile. She'd been fifteen, all knees and with a silly grin.

Katie never looked at the portrait without feeling loved.

"Your grandfather took that?" Josh nodded toward the picture.

"Yes," she responded, grabbing a peach bra from where it hung limply from the bedroom doorknob and shoving it into the drawer of an end table.

"It's very good," he commented, still studying the photograph.

Katie straightened as he swung around to face her.

"You're not giving up on this studio thing, are you?"

"No," she said firmly, pleased that he'd at last recognized how important it was to her.

"And you're not going to go away and leave me in peace anytime soon, either?"

"I need you to give me some time to pay back the loan," Katie returned, hearing the apologetic note in her own voice.

"So you've said." Josh glanced back at the portrait on the wall. "Well, I'll give you six months—"

"You will?" she interrupted him with a squeal.

Josh raised a hand. "But I have a condition."

"Anything," she assured him rashly.

He cocked an eyebrow at her, a sardonic smile curling his lips. "You'd deserve it if I held you to that."

"Well, almost anything," Katie amended quickly.

"First off," Josh said, "do whatever you want with the studio. I'll give you six months to begin making the payments on the loan again. I don't really care how you manage. I'm predicting failure, but it's nothing to me. Starting a small business with no business experience and little photographic experience—"

"I know, I know," she cut him off. "But I can do this. I know I can."

"Secondly, and most important"—Josh strolled closer—"you have to do something for me."

"Okay," Katie said slowly, growing warmer as several immediate possibilities presented themselves.

"Since you canceled my escort this evening," he said, "and assumed that position yourself, I'll want you to be available for future business affairs."

"But you don't think I'm quote unquote presentable enough," she reminded him saucily. "Doesn't it worry you that my Flanagan spontaneity might offend your stuffy conservative associates?"

"Yes, that possibility does concern me. But you've managed to ingratiate yourself with the Williamses—"

Katie giggled.

"—and I have other occasions where I'll require an . . . accessory."

"An accessory?"

"Yes," he said with a sardonic quirk of his mouth. "A young, sexy woman on my arm who bows to my every whim and expects nothing from me in return."

"I can't promise to bow to your whims!" she shot back. "Some of them are stupid."

A steely light dawned in his eyes. "You behaved yourself very well tonight. If you think you can manage to do that on several other upcoming occasions, you have a chance to play at photography in your grandfather's studio. I'll give you six months. If you don't like this bargain, then forget the studio."

That was *all?* Go out with him for business dinners and he'd extend the loan? It sounded too good to be true.

"Oh! You mean you want me to act like I'm in love with you for *social* things?" Katie said, a huge sense of relief prompting her sense of humor to peek out. "I don't mind doing that once in a while. Tonight was fun."

She brushed a hand over her knit skirt. "But I can't promise to dress this well frequently. I borrowed this dress for tonight."

"We don't need to worry about that just now," he told her. "There is, however, one more little thing."

Katie glanced up, feeling triumphant and mischievous. "What? You want me to shine your shoes?"

"No." Josh reached out, brushing his hand along her bare arm before pulling her up against his body.

She looked up at him, a wave of awareness swamping her body as he leaned in to kiss her, his lips taking hers in a move that was more hunger than technique. Hot and fierce, his mouth moved against hers. Katie felt herself suddenly drawn into his lush seduction, tumbling down, immersed in longing and desire.

The scent of him surrounded her as the power of his arms held her against his chest. There was heat everywhere; his mouth branded her and the breadth of his shoulders cast shadows against her eyelids. She felt herself enclosed by darkness, sinking into him, each brush of his lips stirring a thundering in her blood.

Josh opened her mouth beneath his and slid his hands down her back. She felt the sweep of him, his hands large and powerful on her body, urging her closer just as his mouth entreated her to yield her soul.

Grasping the lapels of his dinner jacket, Katie clung to him, lost to the fire raging inside her. Conscious of his touch, the press of his arousal against her belly, she arched back as he trailed kisses down her neck and pressed his heated mouth against the tender spot above her heart.

He cupped her bottom, still pressing her against him with one hand, his other fondling her breast through the soft material of her dress.

Katie moaned, her mouth feeling bruised and tender with his kiss, her body flaming in a riotous chant, calling him, wanting him.

Josh lifted his head and again melded her mouth with his, a softer, sweeter kiss as his hands slid to support her back. She felt his withdrawal with a whimpering need, an agonizing sense of incompleteness.

Slowly he pulled away, his arms still encircling her.

"The . . . last condition," he said, his voice thick, his eyes dark with desire. "No more teasing unless you're offering. I'm likely to take the next invitation you extend without asking any questions."

Four

Katie adjusted the lens aperture on her old Pentax and squeezed off a shot of the girl in front of her.

Framed by the drift of honeysuckle behind her, Camille looked up into the camera, her eyes wide, a hint of hesitation on her face. At almost sixteen she was on the verge of womanhood, poised delicately on the brink of emotions and relationships she didn't yet understand.

Not that additional years would add to her understanding much, Katie thought, remembering Josh and their heated kiss. Heck, she didn't really like the guy much, which made it even more annoying that his kiss packed such a wallop.

She shifted the camera in her hands and sized up the picture in front of her. Capturing this fragile moment in Camille's life was Katie's challenge this morning—not figuring out Josh. That was the reason she'd brought her subject to the park. Camille's parents wanted a portrait for the girl's sixteenth birthday and Katie hadn't yet learned to use the computerized camera in the studio.

She shifted again in the dewy grass to size up a different angle.

All morning she'd thought about the deal she'd made with Josh, wondering what she'd let herself in for. Socializing with him and his stuffy business associates while pretending to be his girlfriend? It didn't sound all that exciting—except for that kiss. Of course, Josh hadn't left her a lot of choice. My-way-or-the-highway Josh. He definitely didn't need lessons in delivering ultimatums.

"Camille," she said, dragging her mind back to the session, "tell me about your classes in school. I get nervous when people sit quietly while I'm working."

"Oh, okay." Elf-slender in her floaty dress, the girl had the dark hair, blue eyes and fair skin of the Irish. She would photograph superbly if Katie could get her to relax.

"I'm in the tenth grade," she said, shooting Katie and the camera another nervous glance. "I have the usual classes. You know, like, English and algebra, history and all that stuff."

"I guess the best part of school is hanging out with your friends," Katie said, remembering well her own high school days.

"Yes." Camille's shy smile lit up the viewfinder. "My three best friends and I have been, like, in school together since elementary."

"That's neat." Clicking the shutter several more times, Katie moved to the side. "So are all the boys in tenth grade still goofy?"

The girl giggled before agreeing. "Yes. And the ones who aren't goofy are, like, stuck on themselves."

"What is it about guys?" Katie complained, walking behind the girl so Camille had to look over her shoulder.

"I don't know. They're either asking dumb questions or, you know, calling on the phone to complain about other girls."

"Do you get to date now that you'll be sixteen?" Katie climbed on a nearby tree stump.

"I guess," Camille said, uncertainty darting across her face. "I'm not sure I will, though. I mean, like, the guys who'll ask me are not all that interesting, you know?"

"It always seems that way," Katie agreed, not allowing herself to think of Josh as she lowered the camera long enough to pick up a big, flouncy feather she'd brought along. The soft, muted blue color matched Camille's eyes exactly.

"Here, hang on to this for me," she said casually before climbing back up on the tree stump. "There was this guy in my school who all the girls wanted to go out with. He was a jock, I guess. I could never get why they'd want to stand in line."

"I know!" The light in Camille's blue eyes kindled in agreement. "And they expect girls to do that, you know. Like, faint if they ask them out."

"Men are disgusting," Katie declared with relish, focusing in on the girl's face.

"Completely," Camille agreed, caught up in the subject. "We've got this jock in our school. Derek. He drives, like, this hot convertible and walks through the halls like he thinks he's God's gift."

"What a jerk." Katie crept closer. "Can you bring the feather up to your face like you're hiding behind it?"

"Sure," Camille said absently before continuing, "this guy is so stuck on himself, he acts like he rules the school."

"Guys like that need someone to teach them a lesson." The shutter clicked and a small whirring sound followed as the film was automatically advanced.

She'd love to teach Josh a thing or two about humility. Who did he think he was, kissing her like that and then telling her she'd better watch out and not ask for what she didn't want.

Camille grimaced, the feather resting against her creamy cheek. "It would have to be a pretty big lesson."

"What he needs," Katie said, framing her next shot, "is a girl who turns him down for the prom."

Camille laughed, pleasure lighting her face at the thought, the feather's soft fronds brushing against her rosy lips. "That would be, like, great, but he's so cute, I don't think anyone would turn him down for the prom."

"Not even you," Katie said gently, her finger poised on the shutter.

An arrested expression, full of mystery and admission, changed Camille's face. "No. I don't think even I would turn him down."

Katie snapped the shutter, capturing the moment.

"Hang on a second." She straightened, excitement bubbling inside her as she climbed off the tree stump to get a new roll of film. That last shot was priceless, full of the contradictions of teenagehood. She'd known this kid would photograph like a dream.

Regardless of what Josh Morgan thought, she had a knack for this, a feel for portraiture that she'd learned from watching her grandfather all those weekends and summers.

Crossing a grassy patch to where her camera bag sat, she noticed for the first time that she'd attracted several onlookers. A small group of well-dressed women stood on the path that cut through the wooded section of the park, watching the session.

To her surprise, one of them waved at her, leaving the path as the others walked on.

It was Madison Williams. Josh's boss's young wife.

"Katie," Madison said excitedly as she crossed the grassy area, "I couldn't believe my eyes when I saw you there working."

"Hi, Madison," she said, remembering Josh's statement that this woman's husband was important to his career and then banishing the concern completely. "I didn't expect to see you here, either."

"I belong to a volunteer club," Madison said with a smile. "We meet in the garden room over at the botanical center at the edge of the park."

"Oh!" Katie smiled back, absurdly pleased that this beautiful, slightly lost young woman had something else going on in her life besides her obnoxious older husband. "That sounds like fun."

"Sometimes it is," Madison agreed before glancing to where Camille waited. "I'd love to see the proofs of this session. Your subject seems so relaxed and comfortable, as if she's not even aware that you have a camera in your hand."

Katie laughed. "That's the idea. If I can get her to be less self-conscious, all her natural beauty shines through and the photos will be good. It always works that way."

A thoughtful look descended on the other woman's face. "Yes, I'm sure that's so. But most people are probably comfortable with you."

"Th-thank you," Katie stammered, surprised by the compliment.

"You have a natural warmth about you. You're friendly," Madison went on, "and you act like people interest you."

"Well, they do," Katie agreed, her habitual buoyancy reasserting itself.

"I have an idea," Madison pronounced. "I want you to do our annual club photos. The photographer we used last year took posed, stiff pictures. I'm sure you can do better."

"Thank you!" Katie said with excitement. "I'd love to do it."

"I'm on the yearbook committee," Madison said, "and I'm sure they'll vote with me on this. Let's make an appointment for them to look over your portfolio."

Josh walked into the country club banquet room, hastily tugging the sleeve of his dinner jacket down over his cuff. He'd come straight from work, changing in his office so he wouldn't be late. The dinner this evening for all the assistant vice presidents, general managers and vice presidents was to celebrate their making their target sales goal for the last six months.

Managing his contribution to the accomplishment had taken a lot of work, but evenings like this weren't purely a reward. He'd long ago come to realize that business social events were still business events. The country club's quietly expensive decor and the tables gleaming with cutlery and crystal proclaimed the tone of the evening. He supposed the trappings of success inspired employee incentive.

He glanced around the room, noting that Dave Williams sat at one of the tables near the front. Next to him sat his young wife in a slender black dress, her dark hair swept elegantly off her neck, discreet pearls at her ears. The place was filled with employees and their spouses.

For a second Josh felt conspicuously alone and was glad he'd had his secretary notify Katie of the evening's event. She was a pain, but having her beside him would unquestionably raise his stature with some of the people who mattered. He felt silly playing games like this. Still, having Katie here and sparring with her covertly would help dissipate his almost certain boredom.

Josh paused in the doorway, his body tightening suddenly with a remembrance that was the antithesis of boredom. Who'd have thought coltish Katie Flanagan would make such a satisfying armful? Those soft full lips had nearly driven him to distraction.

Would she come tonight?

Plastering a smile over his uncertainty on that question, he moved through the tables, searching for someone in his group. He was betting on Katie coming through for this one, if only because Flanagans knew where their best interests lay. If she wanted the studio, she had to play it his way.

At a table off to his right, he saw Rick waving him over.

"Hey, Josh buddy!" the other man called in a low tone. "Come join us."

Seated next to Rick was a petite blond woman who exuded both elegance and money from the top of her feathery hair to what he could see of her classic navy evening dress.

She smiled at Josh brightly.

"This is Melissa Mangrum," Rick said, lifting his eyebrows as he made the introduction.

Corporate arm décor.

Ignoring the message his friend was telegraphing, Josh greeted the attractive woman. Rick was apparently getting

a head start on impressing the management with his own
ability to fit in with the players in this game.

A sudden flash of red-gold hair by the door caught
Josh's attention and he turned, seeing Katie make her way
through the group.

Thank God. She was here and on time.

Relieved she'd measured up to his expectations in this,
at least, he walked to meet her as she made her way
through the group of dinner-jacketed men gathered by the
door.

Then the group of men parted and Katie came more
fully into view.

Josh stopped in his tracks. Damn. Why hadn't he
thought to mention that while the dinner required formal
attire, gold sequin wasn't the look he had in mind?

He should have known better than to rely on Katie
Flanagan.

She was gold from head to toe. Her curly red hair was
piled on her head in wild abandon. That he could live with.
But the rest of Katie radiated the brilliance of an Oscar
look-alike contestant.

Gold sequins and beads clung to her slender body as if
they had been glued on. Molded low over her cleavage,
swirling down over her rib cage to cling to her hips, the
damn dress dripped gold. From décolletage to the brief
skirt, she looked to have been gold-plated. Then there
were the stockings. Those long, sexy legs were encased in
sheer hose that glittered gold over her skin. She even had
gold slipper sandals on her feet.

Josh felt himself flushing with annoyance and embarrassment as the coworkers seated at tables around him
began to murmur, heads turning her direction.

Crap.

What the hell had he been thinking when he'd asked Katie Flanagan, of all people, to help him up the career ladder? She was a Flanagan, for God's sake. Katie, the wildest, least reliable one of all. What the hell did she know about discretion or elegance?

How stupid could he get?

Her outfit stood out in this black-clad group like a loud noise in a convent.

"Hi," she said, glancing around the room with interest. "This is a really nice place. I didn't know you corporate clones got treated so well."

"Be quiet," he said through his teeth, forcing his lips into a plastic smile to hide his frustration with her. Had she done this deliberately? Set out to make them both look like fools?

Determinedly ignoring the stares directed at Katie, he put his hand on her elbow and steered her toward their table.

It wasn't like he could eject himself or Katie out of this scenario. She was here—dressed like a high-priced street-walker—and he had to make the best of it.

But he heard the snickering, saw the disbelieving stares. Someone behind him made a murmured comment that set the whole table guffawing.

Hardening his jaw, Josh pulled out a chair for Katie to help seat her at their table.

"Well, hello," Rick said. "I'll bet you're Josh's date for the evening.

"This is Katie Flanagan." Josh made the introductions, his voice tight. "Rick Goring and his date."

"Melissa Mangrum," the elegant blonde supplied with a smile even more plastic than Josh's.

"Nice to meet you," Katie said, offering her own, more genuine greeting.

"Nice to meet *you*," Rick responded, managing to leer briefly in her direction before shooting his friend a sympathetic glance.

"What a . . . lovely dress," Melissa said, her smile faintly tinged with contempt. "I don't think I've seen one like it."

"Thank you." Katie's response was more hesitant, as if she were picking up the other woman's bitchy undertone. Hell, she couldn't help but pick it up, Josh thought.

The sudden self-consciousness on her face caught his attention. So she *hadn't* deliberately set out to create a stir. This debacle was accidental then, and completely Flanagan-like, but no less embarrassing to him.

Seating himself next to her, Josh quickly began offering the wine that sat in the center of the table. He had figured that even Katie would know how to dress herself appropriately. But despite his frustration at being made a laughingstock in front of his friends and boss, he found himself feeling an unexpected pang of sympathy for his date.

Katie sat next to him quietly, her usually brilliant smile dimmed as the others at the table talked.

He saw her covert glances at the more conservatively dressed people seated around them, and slowly, he saw the consternation spring into her eyes. For some reason, that made him even more irritated at the tittering and staring. Yes, she wasn't dressed appropriately, but who the hell did these people think they were to make fun of others this way?

Katie didn't look bad in that dress. Well, yes, she looked *bad,* but only in a way that most men would pay money for. She actually looked damn good. She certainly carried off the look with more success than most women could. Hell, the snippy blonde with Rick didn't have the assets to hold the gold-sequined dress up for more than a minute. No wonder she was showing her claws.

Catching Katie's anxious sideways glance, Josh knew she'd realized the cause of his chagrin. His hissing at her to "be quiet" probably hadn't made her more comfortable, either. To his intense annoyance, a surge of guilt pushed its way past the embarrassment occupying his awareness.

"Would you like some wine?" he asked, his voice softening as he turned to her.

"Um, sure," she said, her cheeks pink with self-consciousness as a couple walked by their table and both the man and woman stared rudely at Katie.

Josh glared at them, feeling suddenly and unwillingly protective of the flustered woman glittering next to him.

As the evening progressed, servers moving busily between the tables, the staring continued. Thankfully everyone was engaged with dinner and most of the people who looked Katie's way restricted themselves to raised eyebrows and small, supercilious smiles.

Rick's date, however, was a witch.

"I noticed your gold hose," she said to Katie once everyone at their table had been served. "Did you get them out of a catalog?"

Katie murmured something unintelligible, her blue gaze flashing briefly toward the other woman before returning to her plate.

"Because I saw them in a catalog once," Melissa

claimed with a malicious smile. "I think it was Frederick's of Hollywood."

"Rick," Josh said, responding to an urge to shield Katie from his date's spiteful tongue, "did you finish going over those sales figures?"

His friend's gaze bounced between the women before he responded to the question. "Yes, I left them with your secretary."

"Good." Josh knew his voice sounded too hearty. "I'll look them over tomorrow and we'll, uh, get together."

The meal seemed to drag on. He counted a total of three comments from the usually exuberant Katie. Twice she agreed to pass the bread to someone further around the table and once she refused more wine.

Josh found himself exhausted as the dinner drew to a close, all his efforts at shop talk dwindling into silence. He just wanted the evening to be over.

This had been a stupid idea from the start. What had made him think that flamboyant Katie Flanagan could ever fit into the corporate world in any way? He'd been an idiot to come up with the scheme. It wasn't like she could make a go of the studio anyway, and clearly she wasn't able to provide him with what he needed in the way of window dressing.

Not that she didn't look fabulous. But rather than reflecting the sheen of macho studly power from his direction, she'd ended up embarrassing them both. They just needed to call this deal off. He didn't want her social missteps to mess up his promotion, and he didn't want her hurt anymore.

With relief, Josh saw Dave Williams go to the podium at the front of the room. There would be a few speeches,

Williams would present a commendation or two and the night would be over.

Everyone turned attentively toward the front.

Sitting at the back of the table, Josh heard his boss joking at the microphone, but his every attention was tuned to Katie, who sat next to him. He was aware of the rigid way she sat in her chair, aware of her twisting the napkin in her lap. The first sparkling tear that fell to the napkin was silent.

She sniffed then—a small, woebegone sniff that acted on his heart in a powerful way. He wanted to beat someone up. Preferably Miss Smirky across the table.

Katie glanced at him a minute or two later, her face reflecting too clearly the misery she felt. She leaned toward him and whispered, "I-I'm not feeling well. I-I think I need to leave."

Looking at her, he saw the damp path of her tears visible along the taut, golden-ivory skin of her cheek and felt the urge to shake her. What the hell had she done that she was so quickly and easily defeated? Where was his spunky Katie? The one who'd made his life with Erin a misery with her taunting and teasing?

Instead of throwing up her head and staring these snobs down, she wanted to tuck her tail between her legs and run. *Flanagan-style,* whispered a disappointed voice in his head. Damn it, running just wasn't an option.

"Did you hear me?" she asked, close enough that he could feel the warmth of her breath on his ear.

"Yes." He met her gaze with a challenge of his own. "This won't last much longer. Stay."

Katie looked at him, tears filling her blue eyes again. "Josh."

The single, whispered word was a plea, but it fell on resistant ears.

"Stay," he said, his voice lowered but implacable. "There's no reason for you to go."

"My dress—" she whispered haltingly

"—Is fine," Josh finished. "Fine."

At the podium, one of his coworkers accepted a commendation. The woman's conservative satin evening suit was so subdued it might as well have been wallpaper. No cleavage, no expanse of bare legs.

"Look at her," Katie murmured, nodding toward the woman who was accepting the award. "That's what I should have worn."

"It wouldn't do you justice," Josh said, not looking away from the speaker. "Stay."

Katie sniffed back a small sob, drawing his gaze back to her face.

"Stay," he said again, meeting her gaze with his own, full of challenge. 'We'll leave when this is over."

She sat back in her chair, still holding his stare. With one slender hand, she brushed at her damp cheek and then turned, looking toward the podium.

As her chin lifted, Josh felt a flash of pride he didn't want to examine too closely.

They walked away from the lights of the country club after the dinner, headed toward Katie's car in the parking lot.

Reaching the small foreign convertible with its banged up fender and listless paint job, Katie turned around to face him, her gold-sequined dress glinting under the parking lot lights.

"This isn't going to work," she said, her flushed face both upset and angry. "I don't fit in with those snobs and they hate me."

Josh laughed without meaning to. "Hate isn't the right word. Try envy."

"Envy?" she gasped. "Did you hear their snide, rude—"

"Some of the women were rude," he said judicially, "but most of the men were drooling and wanting to take you to bed."

"Thanks," she snapped, "but that doesn't make me feel any better. I'm through. I'm not having anything more to do with these people!"

"I'm sorry they upset you," he said, sobering when he saw her distress.

Katie fished a tissue out of her small evening purse and blew her nose defiantly. "This isn't going to work!"

Watching her dry her eyes, Josh silently assessed the situation. Funny how her reaching the same conclusion as he had earlier made him more . . . determined. Following her as she trailed through the parking lot, surreptitiously sniffling back tears, he'd developed a sudden case of obstinacy.

Maybe Katie hadn't aced this first test of her accessory role, but it went against his grain to give up so easily on anything. If his promotion had been at serious risk because of this one goof-up, he'd have felt differently about it, no doubt. But while her overly gold, overly sexy dress had been out of place, her stunning good looks could only have done him good in the male hierarchy of sexual power.

"It is going to work," he declared abruptly. "People have short memories about things like this.

"Josh! Give it up!" she snapped. "can't you see I'm not good at this?"

He frowned at her, annoyed at how easily *she* gave up and irritated with her for giving herself so little credit.

"No, I don't see that," he denied, feeling even more stubborn. For once, he wanted to see a Flanagan stick to something. "What I see is that we need to put some more effort into making the plan work."

The next evening, Josh closed the hotel room door and dropped his briefcase and laptop computer onto the desk.

He had work to do before his meetings tomorrow, but he wouldn't be able to concentrate now. Learning at ten in the morning that he had to be in another city by eight o'clock that evening tended to leave him feeling a tad wound up.

How exactly had he been tapped for this pain-in-the-ass assignment anyway? Cleveland, Amarillo and Denver in three days. Whooeee. Big-time fun.

Shrugging out of his suit jacket, he opened the minibar without hesitation and downed half of a bottled water. What did it matter if the damned thing cost three bucks?

This trip sucked.

Here he was on a spur-of-the-moment journey, picking up after someone else's screw-up. Alone in a motel room in a strange town at eight o'clock at night.

Of course, the company didn't care that he'd had plans—tickets to a ballgame with some friends this evening. Tomorrow he was to have taken Katie to dinner to give them a chance to go over some of the finer details of the role she'd reluctantly agreed to continue fulfilling.

He'd been right to insist on it. At work the next day, three different men had made envious comments about her. They'd not unnaturally assumed Josh had been well taken care of by his luscious date.

If only he'd been so lucky.

Instead, he'd gone home alone and lain in bed remembering her slender body in that damn dress and the way she'd felt in his arms when he'd kissed her.

No, he wasn't giving up on the plan yet, for lots of reasons. Still, Josh didn't want her embarrassed again. It had been stupid of him not to have given her a more detailed understanding of his world in the first place. After all, she'd never come close to being involved in corporate culture before.

But their dinner would have to be rescheduled. He was here instead, tending to a business crisis that demanded his complete attention. Tomorrow.

Tonight, it was him and the four walls.

If he'd been a drinker, he would spend the next six hours bouncing through Cleveland's bars. But he had meetings beginning at practically sunrise, and he'd never been a fan of hangovers or tawdry one-night stands.

An image of Katie flashed through his mind then. Katie in her sizzling gold dress, her chin still lifted as they had exited the country club. Despite the glitz to her outfit, there was nothing tawdry about the woman. She'd displayed an unexpected class that evening.

If she'd been here with him, he thought, he could have found an endless number of ways to keep them both entertained. But business travel was defined by its solitary nights, and his relationship with Katie was purely a matter of convenience on his side and finances on hers.

No matter how damn sexy she was or how her sultry smile had taken possession of his dreams.

Draining the bottle of water, he opened the cabinet that held the television and retreated to the bed, remote in hand. There was no barhopping, no Katie to rouse and exhaust his body. Nothing much but the tube to fill the hours stretching ahead.

Sometimes this job sucked.

Josh clicked on the television, reflecting on the demanding aspects of his job. Late evenings at the office were the norm and he usually brought home tasks that he didn't get to during the hectic hours of the workday. Such was the downside of success. At this level, it required complete commitment, complete focus.

The VP level demanded even more. More time, more energy.

Flipping through the television channels, he thought of Michael, a coworker, who'd up and quit last year. He'd been a damn good general manager. Everyone had liked him, but he'd just walked in one day and resigned. Just like that. Walked out on a promising career in midstream.

Later he'd tried to explain it to Josh, using terms like "burned out" and "insane work load." Of course, Michael had a wife and kids. The children were growing up without him, he said, because he spent 75 percent of his life on the job.

So he quit and went into consulting.

Josh couldn't imagine a more risky, uncertain choice, particularly for a family man. Sure, consultants could make good money, but self-employment brought a kind of roller-coaster rhythm. Feast or famine. And sometimes the famine lasted months, even years.

It wasn't for him—no matter how many damn trips the company sent him on.

The phone rang just then and he stretched to pick up the receiver.

"Hello."

"Hey, buddy. Guess you made your flight," Rick said. "Unless you ran to Cleveland. The way you were speeding around the office today, you looked like you could have beat the plane."

"Hi, Rick," Josh said, the sound of his friend's vibrant voice making him notice how tired he was. "Yeah, I got here."

"Better you than me," Rick admitted. "That's one thankless mess Dave handed you."

"Nothing new there." Josh put up a hand to rub his eyes. "Did you remember to fax that contract to the Cleveland office?"

"Yes," Rick said. "And I called to confirm that someone picked it up from the fax machine. So you should be good to go tomorrow."

"Thanks, buddy. I appreciate it."

"No problem. So you're hitting Amarillo and Denver after your meetings in the morning?"

"Yes." Josh could feel himself sinking lower and lower onto the mattress, his fatigue increasing exponentially as he thought about the next three days.

"You'll handle everything," his friend told him confidently. "And you know what this trip means."

Josh lifted his head, adjusting the phone against his ear. "What?"

"You got this for a reason," Rick said with a chuckle. "They're testing your commitment, son. Throw that dog a stick and see how fast and how well he fetches it."

He was right, Josh recognized, propping himself up on his elbows. "Yeah, well, I've got my eye on the stick and it's mine."

Rick laughed again. "Like I said. You'll handle it."

Several minutes later, Josh hung up the phone, his exhaustion lifting as a new sense of purpose brought him to his feet. He clicked off the television.

Rick was right. He'd been sent to handle this mess and Williams and the other VPs would be watching the outcome carefully.

He was so close, he could smell success.

Five

No, he wasn't thrilled to be here in a strange town, Josh admitted to himself. He hadn't been eager to cancel his plans. But a few missed ball games and lonely nights weren't too big a price to pay for security—to never again in his life be without the means to take care of himself. When he eventually had a family, he'd make sure they were well provided for against an uncertain future.

He realized now that part of the reason he'd made such a stupidly noble gesture as to offer marriage to Erin when she was pregnant and abandoned was his longing to have a family again. They'd only dated a few times when she'd realized she was pregnant by a former lover. But when she'd admitted her predicament to Josh, he'd almost immediately fallen in love with the idea of an instant family. Like a fool.

Josh went to the small desk and opened his briefcase. This wasn't the time for him to be lounging in front of the television. He should be lining up his strategy for the meeting in the morning.

As he shuffled through his materials, a single sheet of notepaper drifted out and fell back into the case. Katie's phone number. He'd left in such a hurry, he hadn't had time to call her and reschedule their dinner. He'd brought her number along, intending to phone her from Cleveland.

A smile curved his mouth as he thought about Katie, wondering what she was doing now. Would she be working at the studio? Did she have portrait sittings at night?

He frowned, holding the scrap of paper with her number in his hands as he walked to the phone to call her.

She shouldn't be in the studio alone at night with clients. Women had to be very careful these days. He'd have to ask her about that. She was such an airheaded, trusting soul, she'd probably let anyone in the door.

Of course, bad things happened to women in the daylight hours as well. She should probably hire a receptionist to work when she has appointments scheduled, just for safety's sake.

Josh sat down on the bed and lifted the telephone receiver, punching in her home number. He hadn't thought to bring the studio's number and he wasn't even sure she had a working phone there.

Waiting while her home phone rang, he conjured up a picture of her in his mind: slender and shapely, the tumble of her red-gold hair waving around her shoulders.

God, the woman kissed like a fantasy.

Just remembering their one embrace left his body tightened, his breath hard in his throat. She wasn't home, he realized on the sixth or seventh ring. No answering machine clicked on to take his message.

Damn. Disappointed, Josh hung up the receiver and sat staring into space with a frown as he wondered where she might be this late in the evening.

What the heck was the woman up to? Did she stay out

late every night? Partying? Club-hopping with her friends?

Trying to remember the last name of her friend Bethany, he stretched his hand out to pick up the phone again when realization slammed into him with the force of a sledgehammer.

What the heck was *he* doing? Whatever Katie was up to at nine-thirty in the evening wasn't his business. She was the most flighty and unreliable of all the Flanagans he knew. Of course, she was out doing something completely off the wall. Hell, just two days ago, she'd tried to run out on his business dinner because she'd embarrassed herself.

That's how Katie handled things. She ran.

Still, what she did outside of their deal had nothing to do with him.

He dropped the paper with her phone number on the nightstand and went back to his briefcase, appalled at how quickly he'd lost sight of his primary goal this evening. How easily he'd begun to slip into assuming responsibility for keeping Katie Flanagan on track.

Unquestionably, the woman was a massive distraction to him. Yes, she fired his libido like few women ever had, but that sexy, silly spirit of hers teased at him and almost made him lose sight of what was important.

She was an unreliable, unstable firecracker in his hand and he'd better damn well remember the perfidy of which Flanagans were capable.

It wasn't acceptable, this impulse to get closer to her. He'd either have to grow a thicker skin when it came to Katie's charms or seduce the woman into his bed long enough to get her out of his head.

He wasn't even back to the desk when the hotel phone rang again.

"Hello?" he said, stepping back to the nightstand to answer it.

"So it *was* you calling," Katie said, in a self-congratu-latory tone. "I thought so when I saw the long-distance phone number on my caller ID. Give a girl time to get out of the shower before you hang up."

Josh sank onto the bed, swallowing hard against the tightness in his chest at the image her words conjured up. A damp, naked Katie holding the phone to her ear.

"Sorry," he paused, saying gruffly, "do you need to . . . dry off or something?"

Her soft laughter trickled through the telephone line, raising the hairs on the back of his neck. "No. I'm fine. Where are you? When I hit call return, I heard the hotel operator give the name, but not the city."

"Cleveland." For some damn reason, hearing her honey-warm voice as he was standing in this strange hotel room thousands of miles away from home left him feeling oddly tongue-tied.

"Good grief! Did you tell me you were going out of town?" she asked. "It must be a quick trip if we're having dinner tomorrow night to plan our campaign to win your promotion."

"I won't be able to make tomorrow night," he said automatically, some part of his brain registering her use of the term "our campaign" with a strange surge of warmth.

"Oh."

Was that disappointment in her voice?

"It was a sudden trip," he said quickly. "I didn't know

I was going until this afternoon. We'll get together when I get back on Friday, if that's good for you."

"Fine," she said, her natural vivacity returning.

"I'll call you and . . . I'm sorry about interrupting your shower."

"Not a problem," she assured him with a hint of laughter. "Well, good night."

"Good night."

Josh hung up the phone, staring at the instrument for several long minutes before shaking off his abstraction and returning to his work with more energy than he'd felt all day.

She still couldn't believe she'd gotten the job. Katie drove to the women's club building with dollar signs dancing in front of her eyes. There were actually people who agreed with her that she could do this! Of course, she'd done several smaller jobs already, but all of her clients so far had been friends who were willing to give her a chance because they were friends. This job was awarded by complete strangers totally on the basis of her ability.

She could hardly wait to wave that under Josh's disbelieving nose.

Madison Williams had called just yesterday with the news that the women's club yearbook committee had loved her portfolio and wanted her to start immediately. With a club membership of over forty women of means, this contact would lead to bigger and better things, she was sure.

Katie left her small compact car in the lot next to the

park, bounding excitedly across a charmingly rustic bridge to the club building.

This job couldn't have come at a better time. After that disastrous dinner with Josh's coworkers, she'd felt smaller than a freckle on a ladybug. Her only consolation that night had been her previously unsuspected ability to stick it out in the face of the mocking glances and taunting comments.

At Josh's insistence, she'd stayed until the evening was over, stood firm in the face of humiliation. But she hadn't enjoyed it.

The women had looked at her like she was scum and the men had been even worse. They'd looked at her like scum they could sleep with.

If she never saw that witchy crowd of men and women again, she'd count herself blessed. Only, of course, she was bound to have to see them again. After that awful dinner, she had no idea why Josh was holding her to their deal. But if she wanted him to be reasonable about the studio, she had to accompany him to his stupid business events.

For an instant, she remembered the loneliness she'd thought she heard in his voice when he'd called her last night. The emotion seemed strangely un-Josh-like and if the man were lonely, wouldn't he go find a real "corporate girlfriend" instead of coercing her into the role?

But if this was the way he wanted it, fine. As disastrous as that last event had been, she couldn't understand why he wouldn't give up on his plan. Unless it was just plain stubbornness. When he'd become engaged to Erin, she thought he must have been a glutton for punishment, and now she saw just how true her assessment had been.

Katie grinned as she opened the heavy plate-glass door to the club building. The last two days, she'd spent many an hour planning the outfit she'd wear the next time she met up with Josh's work people. Something slit up to her thigh, preferably in silver and scarlet with a neckline that plunged to her waist.

The witches of the corporate world could choke on their disapproval, she thought gleefully.

"Katie!" Madison met her just inside the door. "Come in. I'm so excited that you could come today. We usually meet on Tuesdays and I wanted to introduce you to everyone so they will know you when they schedule their appointments for their sittings."

Madison led her into a large room furnished like the lobby of a posh hotel with beautifully upholstered chairs sitting in groups around tables. There must have been a half-dozen large arrangements of fresh flowers scattered around the room, most of them with subtle touches of burgundy to match the heavy drapes at the windows.

Eager to meet the women she'd be working with, Katie smiled at the chattering group . . . and immediately recognized three women from Josh's dinner.

Good grief.

She halted just inside the door, scanning the group of well-dressed, polished women. They all looked the same, all dressed in the latest trends, all with hair styled by the hand of an expert. All wearing jewelry that would pay her rent for six months.

The wives and daughters of the men at that dinner the other night.

What the heck had Madison gotten her into? She was supposed to photograph *these* women? The ones who had snickered at her behind their manicured hands while their husbands had sized her up for a quickie?

"Uh, Madison?"

But the other woman was several steps ahead, greeting an older woman whose perfectly arranged blond hair and painfully slender figure belied the telltale signs of age on her face.

"Katie," Madison said, drawing her forward gracefully, "I'd like you to meet Susan Chapman. Her husband is the CEO of Chapman Oil."

"Nice to meet you." Susan Chapman's handshake was surprisingly firm for a woman who looked like she'd blow away with the slightest puff of wind. But despite the suspicious tautness of the skin over her cheekbones, here was a woman who looked old enough to have helped boost her husband up the ladder of success.

"Hello," Katie said, liking the woman's open smile.

Susan shifted closer, a naughty twinkle in her eye. "So you're the young woman who lit up the room at the Blue Plains Country Club the other night?"

Katie felt her heart stutter. "Excuse me?"

"I've heard all about you." Susan gestured toward another woman standing at Katie's elbow. "Paige's husband works with your fiancé."

Off balance and unsure how to react, Katie glanced at Paige to find the other woman smiling and nodding. *Her fiancé?*

Opening her mouth to correct the woman that she was only *dating* Josh, she found herself cut off.

"We've known Josh forever," Paige said eagerly. "When can I arrange to sit for you? I can hardly wait to see what you'll do with me! I heard your portfolio was great. Someone with your artistic flair can hardly help but do exciting work."

"Artistic flair?" Katie echoed, distracted from the clarification of her exact relationship with Josh. She was beginning to sense that the mood of this group was very different from the hostility she'd picked up the night of Josh's dinner.

"Of course." Madison nodded happily. "We're all so ordinary and boring, we have to play it safe fashionwise. But with your coloring—all that wonderful hair—and your eye for style, you can be daring. Like wearing the gold dress the other night."

"I'll bet you set their tongues wagging," Susan said, chuckling.

Madison giggled, teasing, "You wouldn't believe! She looked so good in that dress! There were several women who were so jealous, they were planning on jumping her in the ladies' room. But I told them Katie's an artist. She practically can't help being noticed."

"Thank you," Katie said faintly, still in shock. They'd thought it was her "artistic flair" that led her to wear the gold-sequined gown? She bit her lip, containing her laughter with an effort. What would they say if she told them she'd found the dress in a resale shop at the last minute and had bought it because it was cheap and had fit her?

"Do you take pictures like that woman who works with babies?" another woman asked eagerly. "I'd like to be photographed just wearing feathers or something exotic like that."

"We can do feathers," Katie said instantly, realizing that these affluent, pampered women were just as excited about having beautiful portraits of themselves as any other woman would be. Some emotional urges cut across money boundaries, apparently.

"I can see Louise in feathers," a dark-haired woman said gaily.

Katie glanced around. All the club members were gathered on this end of the room now, chattering excitedly. What a difference a day or two made. At Josh's dinner, she'd felt glaringly out of place, the focus of many a disapproving stare. Now, the same women welcomed her in anticipation.

"Maybe you could do several shots with her just wearing a single feather or two," someone teased. "That would get John's attention."

The other woman sighed as her friends laughed in good-natured teasing. "What I need is a little of Katie's flair. You know, that cool, I don't care what you think attitude. You were great the other night, Katie. Very regal and sexy at the same time. What man can resist the combination of temptation and aloofness?"

They'd thought she was aloof? Katie looked at the woman, dumbstruck. She'd been so busy trying to hide her embarrassment after Josh insisted she stay until the end of the evening, it hadn't occurred to her that people would misread her emotions.

"We can do temptation and aloofness," Katie said warmly to John's wife. "Leave it to me."

"Really? That would be great! When can we get started?"

Katie rummaged through her bag for her newly purchased appointment book. Things were working out wonderfully! All of a sudden, she had a hundred ideas for different portraits. Sexy, elegant, unique portraits. These women were so sheltered and constrained, even the possibility of displaying some sexual power with their husbands got them excited.

"Wednesday at four." She penciled the woman in. John's wife was named Devyn. Devyn Ford.

The others gathered around her then, clamoring for their appointment times. Confidence and excitement buzzing through her veins, Katie scribbled their names into her schedule, one after another. She could hardly wait to tell Josh.

Mr. Stuffy hadn't thought she could do this. As she finished with the group, another part of her brain kept thinking about how she'd break the news to him, kept picturing the astonishment and chagrin on his face.

He'd done her an inadvertent favor by insisting she stick out that miserable banquet the other night, like a principal disciplining a wayward student. And now she was reaping massive benefits. Maybe playing his little corporate game wasn't such a bad idea, after all.

She could make this work for her. Most small business owners spent major bucks trying to get in with a money crowd, and here was Josh handing her a zillion terrific contacts. These women had children and friends with children. All their husbands needed family portraits on their desks.

Suddenly she had the possibility of more work than she'd dreamed of. Paying work.

Life was very good.

"I'm so excited to have you taking the club photos," Madison said minutes later when the other women had moved away, preparing to leave the meeting.

"Madison," Katie said, shaking the other woman's hand in a surge of gratitude. "Thank you so much for making this possible for me. You're terrific."

Madison flushed, pleasure lighting up her eyes. "I'm glad to help. I know you'll do a wonderful job. Its a win-win situation, as Dave would say."

"Well, I can't tell you what it means to me," Katie replied, putting her book back into her purse.

"I really admire your courage," Madison said suddenly. "I mean, you're really out there taking chances, doing something you really want to do. I-I'm not sure I'd have the guts. I'm too scared of messing up and upsetting people. Scared of making the wrong decision."

Katie frowned, reading unhappiness in her new friend's delicately made-up face.

"I'll tell you a secret," she said wryly. "I'm scared, too."

Madison smiled. "You don't look it."

"Good." She slipped the strap of her bag over her shoulder. "Sometimes you have to fake confidence till the real thing shows up."

"Well, I have confidence in you."

"Thanks," Katie said with another rush of gratitude. She'd originally written Madison off as a beautiful, slightly dim accessory to her husband's success. At first, it seemed as if that must be her only goal in life.

But now Katie was beginning to wonder if the wistful light in Madison's eyes didn't indicate she had some big dreams of her own—perhaps dreams that didn't fit in Dave Williams's world?

* * *

"What do you mean we're going shopping for appropriate clothes?"

Josh looked up from his lunch, meeting her gaze across the table. Their scheduled dinner on Friday had been moved to Saturday lunch when his plane was delayed six hours the day before.

"I mean just what I said. You need clothes appropriate for the social situations I'm putting you into."

"So you have to go with me to buy them?" she asked, her tone both insulted and indignant. "Are you trying to punish me for not correcting the mistake those women at the club made about our being engaged?"

The small restaurant wasn't crowded at lunchtime. Only half the tables were filled with customers. Their table occupied a quiet corner by the window. To anyone observing, it probably seemed like a very peaceful, contented kind of romantic moment between a man and a woman.

Nothing could be further from the truth, Josh thought. "Of course not. We'll just have to deal with that. And yes, I'm going with you to buy clothes. Since you know nothing about this environment and I do, I have valuable input."

"I *saw* what they were wearing!" she said. "Black. A little gray. One woman had on navy, I think."

"It's more than color," Josh said flatly. "I'm coming with you."

Katie trailed behind him as he entered the expensive department store. She probably looked sulky, but who could blame her? What woman could stand a man telling her what to wear? It was impossible!

She'd tried telling him in the car as he drove from the restaurant that the gold dress had really won over the ladies of the country club. Though she secretly knew it was more her snooty way of handling the embarrassing moment that had the women raving about her style, she still resented his saying he wasn't concerned with how her wardrobe impacted *her* business.

He hadn't even congratulated her on her newfound success, the jerk!

Katie's feet sank into the thick pile carpeting as she followed Josh into the evening wear department. Arrogant, stuck-up pain in the neck!

Loitering behind a dress rack as Josh talked with a sales woman, Katie flicked contemptuously through dress after dress.

Black. Every one of them. Some with satin accents. Some with decorative crystal buttons. All of them expensive and subdued.

A rack behind her held pastel versions of the same dresses—a kind of Stepford wardrobe—same kind of cut, same kind of stiff fabrics. Nothing too clingy or sexy. Nothing too revealing. Very mother-of-the-bride. She wouldn't wear this stuff if she were sixty-five!

Not that the store didn't carry more interesting outfits. The entire far section of the finer dresses department held racks of more daring dresses. Many of them were black, of course. But Josh never looked at that side of the dress department.

Was this really what he wanted? A black-wrapped asexual woman as some sort of neutral accessory? She should refuse to do this. The man was autocratic and unreasonable.

Of course, his insisting she stay at the business dinner in her gold dress had inadvertently been a benefit to her. He hadn't meant to help her, but he had. She supposed she ought to give him at least one more chance.

Curious to hear the conversation between him and the saleswoman, Katie drifted closer.

"We'll need half a dozen dresses," he was saying to the woman, looking as comfortable here giving orders as he was in his office. "And I'd like to stay conservative."

"Of course, Mr. Morgan," the saleswoman fawned.

Katie had worked in a store like this once for about three weeks. She knew the sales staff worked on commission and pitied rather than condemned the woman's sycophantic tone. People who shopped in places like this seemed to expect a certain amount of sucking up from sales personnel.

Josh's gaze fell on Katie as she walked reluctantly toward him.

"Probably a size four," he told the woman, as if Katie were a three-year-old unable to speak for herself.

"Size six," she corrected in an annoyed tone. "I'd have to be anorexic to be a four."

The saleswoman smiled. "Why don't I show you to the dressing room and your husband can wait—"

"Fiancé," Josh interjected before Katie could voice the hot correction trembling on the tip of her tongue.

"—fiancé can wait in the sitting area we have just outside the dressing room. You'll have the whole place to yourselves."

On reflection, Katie wasn't sure how she'd have categorized him to the woman except to clarify that he *wasn't* her husband. At this rate, other people would have her bearing children for him before the charade was over.

Still feeling sullen and resisting the urge to scuff her feet like a lagging five-year-old, she allowed the saleswoman to escort her to the dressing room.

Within minutes, the woman returned with an armload of size six black dresses. Here and there, the selection was enlivened by a black number with white touches, and one dress was even a daring rose pink.

Katie shuddered. She wasn't one of those few redheads who could wear pink. The color invariably made her look unwell.

Knowing Josh was outside, sitting in an upholstered armchair in a mirrored alcove, she put on the first dress with mutiny in her heart.

"Come out when you get the first one on, Katie," he called.

Katie stuck out her tongue at her sedate black-clad reflection in the mirror and zipped up the dress before marching to the dressing room door and flinging it open. "Okay, here it is.

Swinging her hips and smiling her sultriest smile at him, she paraded into the mirrored alcove, pausing with her hand on her hip before swinging around like a model on the catwalk.

Josh straightened in his chair, his gaze riveted on her.

With no comment, she turned once more and headed straight back to the dressing room.

"Uh, that was nice," Josh called out, his voice sounding odd as she ripped the sleeveless shift over her head and tossed it over a chair.

The next two dresses were just as boring as Katie strutted out with one, then the other. One was sleeveless and the other had a modest cap sleeve. Other than that, she couldn't really tell the difference between them.

Josh seemed to like them both, however; his attention was fixed intently on her from the moment she opened the door. It was weird, really, because while they were somewhat form-fitting, neither dress revealed much of her.

Black and boring.

On the fourth dress—a tasteful three-quarter sleeve—she threw open the dressing room door and marched out to the raised area in front of the mirrors with no pretense of feminine grace.

"Do you see a trend here?" she demanded, gesturing to the garment covering her. "I refuse to dress like some sort of corporate wife drone! Do these women have opinions? Personal taste of their own? Or are they all privately issued the corporate wife uniform? Is that what we're doing here today? Picking uniforms?"

"Katie," Josh said, visibly battling irritation, "the business world is different. Women are supposed to be attractive without being—"

"Visible?" she snapped, incensed by his obtuse blanket statement. *"Women* aren't just occupying space next to you! We are human beings, each with unique talents and feelings!"

His smile became ironic. "So are the men in the corporate world, honey, but no one cares about our feelings, either."

"What?" She stared at him, his comment taking the wind out of her sails.

"Let me explain." He leaned forward, his elbows propped on his knees, his brow knitted as he formulated his thoughts. "In the weeks ahead, I'll need you to accompany me to several more business dinners, two or three private meals with vendors, and also, help me host a cocktail party at my apartment. On all of these occasions, I'll be just as much on exhibit as will you."

She frowned at him. "You will?"

"Yes." He straightened, an odd quirk to his lips. "I'm up for an important promotion, Katie. I told you that. But part of this business is playing the game. I don't like it any more than you do. Probably less, but if I want to make it to the next level, I have to show the bosses above me that I can work with them, that I understand their values. I have to demonstrate that I'll be a team player."

"And that means not having any individuality?" she asked softly.

His answering smile was crooked. "The business world doesn't give a damn about individuality. It rewards conformity."

"And this is a place you want to be? Why?"

Josh leaned back in his chair, his jaw seeming to firm. "Because this world—if you play it right—assures you of a certain financial stability. Even if a branch of the business is phased out, you can find a place at another corporation more easily if you've played the game. Done your work and kept your nose clean."

"And financial stability is that important?"

For a moment, she wasn't sure he was going to answer her. He drew in a breath and let it out slowly.

"What is a man if he can't take care of himself? Or his family? Hell, he doesn't deserve a family if he can't provide. Yes, stability—the ability to put bread on the table—

that's important. Being able to take care of things without having to rely on—"

"Anyone. I understand," she said slowly, remembering Josh's background. The years he'd lived with first one relative and then another. She didn't necessarily agree with him about money being the answer, but she could see why he might feel that way.

She'd never gone hungry, never felt dependent on people who just suffered her presence; but she had known the absence of a parent. That offered a level of childhood angst, right there, and Josh had lost both parents.

He'd been dependent on others at a terribly vulnerable stage of his life and had obviously suffered in the process. So now he was making sure he could always take care of himself. Never need anyone. Never let anyone close enough to disappoint him.

Like Erin had when she'd dumped him for his own brother when Josh had just been trying to help her out.

"Okay," Katie said, trying not to show the wash of tenderness his unconscious revelation sent over her. "But I'm here for a reason, right?"

"Yes," he said slowly, a cautious glimmer in his face.

"An accessory, you said. Like Madison is Dave's trophy wife?"

"Yes."

She made a puzzled face at him. "Then shouldn't I look a little sexy? I mean, aren't I supposed to show that you're king of the jungle and able to get all the really hot babes?"

"I . . . guess," he said, even more slowly, a smile glimmering in his eyes.

"Then we've got to go for a little more pizzazz," she said, gesturing toward her reflection in the bank of mirrors. "Black makes me look like death. Can't we do chocolate-brown or green or something? And am I allowed to show a little cleavage? Wouldn't it up your jungle rating to attract a woman with boobs?"

Josh smiled before his brows twitched into another frown. "Look. I'm not offering you up to all takers. It's not like I'm procuring. I-I don't want to embarrass you—"

"You won't," she assured him with a grin. "I like short skirts."

"—and I don't want to encourage my coworkers to embarrass you, either," he finished, seeming oddly flustered.

"Oh." Katie looked at him, aware of a smile tugging at her lips. Josh felt protective of her. How unbelievably sweet.

He probably knew how seriously sloshed these guys could get. She'd bet, if the last dinner was anything to go on, that some of his coworkers would hit on her despite her now supposed engagement to Josh.

"You're—" He hesitated as if carefully choosing his words. "You're the kind of woman who would look sexy in a feed bag. It's not like I need to package you just right to show you off."

"Oh," she said faintly, shocked at the compliment. "Okay, I'll wear whatever you think will help."

"Good," he said with obvious relief.

"With two conditions," she said then, her mischievous nature rebounding.

"What?" he asked, foreboding in his face.

"First, we've got to get something besides black and something just a teensy bit more attractive."

"All right."

"And second," she added with an audacious urge to push her luck, "you have to help me this weekend. I need to shoot some photos for my portfolio and I need an extra person."

"I'm not a model," he objected, the frown back on his model-handsome face.

"No?" she echoed with laughing mockery. "Well, that's okay. I actually need some help taking pictures of myself. I need to have different poses for my clients to pick from and since I'm starting from scratch, I have to be my own model."

"I don't know anything about photography."

"You don't need to. I just need another pair of hands," she assured him, heading back toward the dressing room. "I'd have asked Bethany, but she's out of town."

"Fine." His voice followed her as she closed the dressing room door. "We have a deal."

"That . . . that's good," Josh said, forcing the massive understatement out through throat muscles that felt paralyzed.

Before him, on a raised bed mounded with cream cushions and a satin comforter, Katie lounged, wearing what looked like a few artfully placed feathers.

He shifted his stance again, praying the lights shining in her direction left him in concealing shadows. If he'd had any idea what she had in mind, he'd have worn his shirt over his jeans. Hell, he'd have found a thousand excuses to avoid doing this. Who needed this kind of torture?

"So, you're going to do boudoir photography with the

members of the women's club?" he asked after clearing his throat.

"Mmm," she agreed, the purring sound in her throat making his hair rise, along with other body parts.

She looked incredibly hot in a completely sexual way, lying there on that satin bed. Hot and welcoming. Seductive enough to have him drooling if he hadn't snapped his mouth shut. Long silky legs and slender, sexy bare feet. Some kind of sheer, filmy baby-doll something edged with feathers cupped her breasts, dipping low to reveal the smooth golden swells.

Josh wanted to kiss her there in the sweet cleft between her breasts. Instead, he squeezed the camera shutter the way she'd taught him.

"I wasn't ready," Katie protested.

"It looked good," he said gruffly, wishing he weren't quite so ready and that she didn't look quite so good.

Her red-gold hair rippled over bared shoulders. He wanted to kiss her there, too—along the indentation above her collarbone and up the column of her graceful neck. To dip into that delicious hollow.

He wanted to take her mouth beneath his again, crush her to him until she moaned his name. He wanted to thrust into her welcoming body hard and fast, until she screamed out his name in pleasure.

Six

"So, Josh," she said, still in that low breathy voice that made him sweat.

"Uh-huh," he replied, squeezing the shutter release again out of sheer nervous tension.

"Why do you need me to do this fiancée thing for you?"

Josh jerked his mind away from what he really needed her to do at that moment and said in a befuddled tone, "What?"

"Why do you need me to be your corporate accessory?" She shifted to another position, the strap of her feather-bedecked nightie sliding off her shoulder.

"Well, you canceled Deidre that night."

Katie glanced up at him with lifted brows. "But even she was just playing a part. Why don't you have a real girlfriend to make you look good."

Fighting the urge to mop his brow, he gruffly asked her to move to another position. While she shifted, he tried not to watch the delectable movement of her unfettered breasts and struggled to clear his lust-fogged brain enough to answer her.

"I don't have time to date," he said finally.

"You're kidding." Katie lay on her stomach facing the

camera, her chin propped on her raised hands. Her long rumpled hair swept forward, framing her face, and her slender legs were crossed in the air behind her. In that girlish position, she looked like every sixteen-year-old boy's fantasy.

God, she looked like his fantasy.

"No," he said with effort, "I put in a lot of hours at work. Not much time for wining and dining. Women expect a certain amount of attention and I can't give much."

"You sound so stuffy when you say things like that," she said, looking into the lens with a teasing, challenging glint.

Josh's squeezing the shutter bulb felt more like a reflex than a voluntary action.

"I'm not stuffy," he said automatically, so aroused he could hardly think. He'd like to show her just how unstuffy he was feeling at this moment.

"What if I moved over here?" Katie asked, sliding back and flipping over so her legs dangled off the bed at an angle, her back arched so that her breasts pouted forward.

"It's kind of—awkward," he said, swallowing hard and tearing his gaze away from her breasts.

"Remember the overhead camera," she murmured. "We need to get some shots with it."

"Okay," he said, his voice sounding rusty. "Where's the shutter release?"

"Just there." She pointed.

Josh found it and pressed the release without looking at her.

When she said nothing, he swung around, glancing at the bed.

"Josh, don't you get terribly lonely?" Katie asked, her voice low, her gaze fixed on the camera above her.

"Yes." He couldn't deny it. Sometimes he longed to come home to a home-cooked meal and the soothing presence of a woman who wanted to hear how his day went.

Hell, forget the meal. Sometimes he wanted to come home to a vision like Katie, a delectable morsel of pure sexuality to drive him wild with passion.

He drew in a ragged breath and tried to tell himself the hot lights were causing the rapid heating of his blood. He couldn't deny she roused him, but he kept telling himself he was strong enough to resist. He placed a high value on being in charge of himself.

"It might look nice," Katie said softly, still not looking at him, "if you could arrange my hair out around me like a sunburst."

I'd have to touch her to do that, was his only coherent thought. Not a good idea.

"Okay," he said, moving toward the bed as if he were in a trance.

She lay back on the bed, smooth golden legs splayed against the creamy silken covers, fire-licked tresses in a tumble around her face and shoulders.

Before he realized it, he found himself at the edge of the bed, his thighs grazing the coverlet, his hand outstretched to her red-gold hair.

Silky and soft, curling around his fingers like a seductress's limbs, her hair mesmerized him.

Josh looked down into her face, her wide blue eyes meeting his, and he felt himself falling. The world tilting around him, he leaned forward over the bed and placed his mouth on hers wide open and hot. He kissed her, his hands fisting in her luxuriant hair as he lost himself in the stroking of her tongue. She curled toward him, her mouth hot and eager beneath his, her hands settling on his shoulders.

He felt her drawing him down to the bed, felt her fiery hunger in their kiss. Not realizing his movement until he felt her half-naked body in his arms, he found himself beside her on the silken coverlet.

Losing himself in her kiss. Slaking a hunger he'd never before let himself feel. Katie. Only Katie. He needed the taste of her on his tongue.

Writhing on the bed beneath the weight of his body, Katie welcomed his tongue into her mouth. So hot and so right was this man's mouth on hers. She'd relived his kiss so many times, felt again the blossoming warmth in her belly, the urge to press closer.

But now with his hands on her body, his lips layering damp kisses on her neck, her shoulders, he made her frantic.

He wasn't stuffy now, wasn't disapproving and angry—just arousing and tantalizing, his broad shoulders looming over her. The press of his body on hers was erotic and consuming. His kiss . . . she could drown in his kiss, in the mating of their mouths.

He'd never been this way before, never before acted as if he were on the verge of losing control.

Control? Josh never lost control. Did he?

Conscious thought slammed into Katie like a blast of cold air. This was *Josh* pressing kisses to the slope of her breast. Josh cradling her hip in his palm. The same infuriating man who'd called her unstable and unreliable just a few weeks ago. The same guy who persisted in throwing her failures in her face and obnoxiously predicted she'd fail again.

This was the guy currently nipping at her neck and stroking his hand along her thigh.

What was she doing!

Furthermore, what did he think he was doing?

"Josh," she mumbled, pushing at his shoulder.

He nuzzled her ear, his hand moving up to palm her breast.

"Josh!" Katie shoved at him and he yielded to her movement, falling back against the bed on his elbow, his eyes still dark with passion.

"What?" he muttered, his voice thick.

"We shouldn't," she said, her words not as forceful as she'd have wished. "We can't."

"God, why not?" he said thickly, bending to kiss her again.

"Because you don't even like me," she said with asperity. "And I'm not sure I like you much, either."

He straightened as if she'd slapped him, his gaze clearing to stare at her.

"Oh," Josh mumbled then, backing off the bed. "Sure, okay."

Scrambling to find a robe to cover herself with, she suddenly felt naked despite the fact that she'd been sprawled on the bed like this in front of the man for over an hour.

"Listen," he said awkwardly, shoving a hand through his rumpled hair as he stood beside the camera. "If you don't, um, need me anymore, I'll be going."

"Okay," Katie said in a small voice, glancing over her

shoulder as she struggled to tie the belt of the short, silky robe around her.

"Fine." His footsteps retreated.

She turned around to see him disappear through the curtained arch.

Sinking to the tumbled bed, Katie tried to quell the sudden, stupid sense of regret at her poorly timed return to sanity.

He was the last man she needed to get involved with. He was righteous, judgmental and annoying. And besides all that, he'd dated her sister. Even though they'd only gotten engaged because Erin was pregnant and alone, for Katie to get involved with Josh kind of felt like stealing her sister's boyfriend.

Katie hesitated. Well, no, maybe not that. Erin and Josh had never been what she'd consider soul mates, and their brief time together had ended with anger more than regret, from what she could see. They'd never loved each other.

Still, Josh and her together?

Who'd have thought stuffy, arrogant Josh could so completely make her lose her mind? Not to mention the disturbing impact he was beginning to make on her heart.

"Hello?" Her voice sounded breathless, as if she'd rushed to answer the phone.

"Katie?" Josh winced as the stupid inquiry popped out of his mouth. He'd know her voice anywhere.

There was a pause on the other end of the line before she finally said, "Josh. Hi."

Was that wariness he heard in her voice? Did she feel like she needed to be cautious with him now? Shoving a hand through his hair, he mentally kicked himself again for his stupidity the previous day. He never should have touched her, never should have taken advantage of the situation even if she had been lying nearly naked on a bed in front of him. She'd asked him to help with her work, not invited him for a sexual romp.

But she responded to your kiss, a voice whispered in his head. Oh, how she'd responded. Sizzled his nerve endings and kept him up all night thinking about her.

He was still walking funny twenty-four hours after he'd left the studio.

Conscious of the silence on the line, Josh cleared his throat and asked, "How are you?"

"Fine," she answered, the usual blithe bounciness absent from her voice. "And you?"

"Fine." His fingers clenched around the telephone receiver, he cursed his inability to find a way to ease through this conversation. He'd called to apologize for getting out of line. How hard was that? The typical adult male had huge amounts of practice in this sort of apology.

"Good," she said, sounding self-conscious herself.

"Is business going well?" he asked suddenly, relieved to have thought of something sensible to say.

"Yes, very well." She hesitated. "As a matter of fact, I'm in the middle of a sitting now."

"Oh? I'm sorry. I'll let you go." Josh closed his eyes, feeling like an idiot. Here she was actively working and he'd called to take up her time blithering like an idiot over what should have been a simple thing.

"Josh?"

"Yes," he answered, grateful he'd thought to close his

office door before making the call. At least, no one could look in and see him making a fool of himself.

"Did you need to talk to me about something?" she said hesitantly. "You called . . ."

"Yes," he replied, manfully stepping forward to take care of business. "I just wanted to apologize for yesterday."

"I, uh . . . yesterday?"

"I took advantage of the situation when we were at the studio. You needed my help and I—I got out of line. I'm sorry. You're very attractive."

"Oh." The word came softly over the telephone line. "That-that's all right."

"Listen," he said, cursing his own awkwardness. "I know you're busy and you need to go, but . . ."

"Yes?" There was a faint lilt to the question.

"I really do like you," he blurted out before he could stop himself. "You said . . . you made a comment about my not liking you. But I do, even when I think I shouldn't."

"Thanks," Katie said with a second's pause. "Thank's a lot. And Josh?"

"Yes?"

"While we're making admissions," she said, a hint of laughter in her voice, "I could have shot those photos without your help."

Josh froze, the phone feeling glued to his ear.

"Bye," she said, the single teasing-soft word followed by a click as she hung up the phone.

Closing his eyes again, Josh let the receiver settle into its cradle. He'd called her to clear his head of the regret that had kept him from staying focused on anything productive this morning. And now whole new vistas of possibilities made work impossible.

Two weeks later, Katie unlocked the door to Josh's apartment and let herself in. She shut the door and stood in the small entry hall, listening to the silence.

She'd never seen his place before and she knew she had to give in to her overwhelming urge to poke around a little. The man was such a maddening mix. Hard as nails one moment, and calling to apologize for "getting out of line" the next.

Josh kept her swinging from annoyance to arousal to tenderness. More than anything, he left her feeling baffled. Surely something here in the place that was his home would give her a clue to understand him better.

Since their incredibly passionate tussle on the bed in her studio, she'd talked to him only twice. The first time, he called to apologize, startling the heck out of her. The cute awkwardness in his voice when he pointed out how attractive she was and the nervous way he'd cleared his throat when he apologized for getting carried away had left her with a lingering determination to kiss him again.

Then he'd called about the cocktail party and had been all business, as if the hot passion they'd shared and his sweet telephone call had never happened.

Sighing, Katie hoisted the hanger holding her outfit for the evening. That was the trouble with Josh. He usually thought of nothing but business. In truth, that was what had startled her when he'd kissed her that day on the satin bed. All this time, she'd been fighting her attraction to him because of his past association with her family.

But in the last few days, she'd realized the debacle with Erin and him had happened a long time ago and since her sister had obviously moved on, it wasn't like she'd be poaching. Not really. Besides, Josh and Erin had never really been a couple.

When Josh had kissed Katie, his hands buried in her hair, she'd had no thought of her sister or what had happened two years before. Josh hadn't seemed to, either. She'd known he found her attractive, but she'd never known him to lose his iron control. The thought made her tremble. She'd made him do that?

The first kiss they'd shared, the kiss the night he'd made her his offer to keep the studio open, hadn't meant much beyond him displaying a don't-tease-me-unless-you're-asking attitude. It was more of a demonstration of power than anything else. Of course, the first kiss had been pretty great itself, even if he hadn't lost control.

Smiling, Katie wandered curiously into the empty apartment. For whatever reason, she wanted to know him better, to gather an impression of who Josh really was as a man.

Interesting and nicely done was her first thought when she glanced into the room. The earth-toned couch and chairs in the living area were a little too matchy for her taste. But she couldn't fault their casual yet clean style, and he'd managed to strike a nice balance between bachelor pad random style and looking like he'd purchased the whole room en suite from the closest furniture store.

The oak kitchen was predictably bare. Josh had assured her the caterer would have plenty of room and, glancing into the utilitarian room, Katie agreed. There was nothing on the countertop but a coffee maker. The man probably wasn't home often enough ever to use the room.

Down a short hall was a powder room, a spare bedroom with severe navy curtains and a master suite done in navy and hunter plaid. Combined with the spacious living area, the apartment itself was as nice as any she'd seen.

Apparently corporate America paid well, she mused, hanging her evening outfit in the closet in the spare room.

Josh's bedroom was nicer and had its own well-lit bathroom, but for once in her life, caution had to be her watch word. That was a strange experience for her, because she usually dove into things, sure she'd find some way to manage. And usually she did. But this relationship felt riskier for some reason, as if more were at stake.

She knew she didn't need to be dressing in Josh's room until she was ready to commit to him on an emotional level. Such intimacy could only lead to other intimacies. Unquestionably, the physical attraction between them hovered near combustion.

A moment's reflection was all it took to remember the strength of his arms around her, the clouded hunger in his eyes. The fluttering, piercing longing in her stomach. She wasn't inexperienced. She'd dated men before, heck, even been engaged a couple of times before, as Josh had so rudely reminded her. Yet this strange inclination for the company of her sister's discarded fiancé brought up a tumult of emotion she couldn't sort out. She wanted to fight with him . . . and at the same time she wanted to make love with him.

But Josh was a man who set up roadblocks to love. He had her inextricably linked with her cheating sister. Letting herself get too close to him felt risky in the extreme.

She'd already gotten lost in his kisses, felt incredibly desired and cherished only to return to reality with a bump. Going there again might sound irresistibly delicious, but she didn't think she should.

Of course, that made her want to all the more.

Still, dressing for the evening's festivities in his masculine bedroom when he could walk in on her was making herself way too available to him.

Just as she was closing the closet door in the spare room, the phone rang.

Katie stepped into the hall, listening for the ring to try and decide which phone was the closest one.

There, in his bedroom.

Hurrying into the room, she spotted the phone beside his bed and threw herself across the king-sized monstrosity to grab the receiver on the fourth ring.

"Hello?"

"Hello," a nasal female voice intoned. "May I speak with Mr. Josh Morgan?"

"He's not here."

"Oh," the woman hesitated. "Well, I left a message at his office and I'd like to leave one with you, as well."

"Okay," Katie said agreeably.

"This is Norton's Catering and we regret that we'll be unable to serve this evening."

"What!" Katie straightened to her knees on the bed. "But you can't! We've got fifty people coming tonight and Josh expects food for them."

"I'm very sorry, miss," the Norton's woman said, not sounding particularly distressed. "The employee who arranged this job with Mr. Morgan failed to write him into the schedule and we only realized it just now. We have four other jobs tonight and we're just not able to do Mr. Morgan's, too."

"Well, send the employee who screwed up and let her do it," Katie declared indignantly.

"I can't do that. She's been fired."

Damn.

"So you're just leaving us high and dry?" Katie's voice rose. "Give me the idiot's phone number and *I'll* make her come do it!"

"I'm very sorry."

"Listen," Katie barked, Josh's voice seeming to channel through her. "It was our understanding that Norton's was a reliable, professionally run business. You made a commitment to us and I demand you honor it!"

Though she'd never heard of the catering company, she knew Josh well enough that she had no doubt he'd gotten referrals and probably a verbal contract before hiring the firm.

"I'm sorry, miss," the woman said, her inflection unchanged. "But there's nothing we can do. Good-bye."

"Wait a minute!" Katie shrieked into the dead phone. "What do you make for fifty people? Crab puffs? Swedish meatballs? Bologna sandwiches?"

The dial tone was as monotonously uninterested as the woman from Norton's had been.

Katie slammed down the phone and vaulted off Josh's bed to pace in front of it. What should she do? He'd sent her over here this afternoon to let the caterers in and be here if they needed anything.

And to think she'd been annoyed with him for treating her like an incompetent idiot! Like she couldn't do anything but "let the caterers in and be window dressing when his office drones arrived. *Just unlock the door for them,* he'd said in that faintly dismissive, patronizing tone of his that made her want to stab him with the closest sharp implement.

Now, just unlocking the door for the caterer sounded really good. She'd have given anything to have nothing to do this afternoon! Maybe she should just leave. She hadn't agreed to cook for a crowd! Most of the time she just barely managed to cook for herself.

Katie got off the bed and headed for the front door. Halfway down the hall, an image of Josh's face flashed in her head. His face when he'd talked so briefly about needing this promotion.

She hesitated, her purse dangling from her hand, indecision halting her. There was nothing she could do about this mess. Not really. And Josh would be upset with her no matter what she did.

Leaving was her best option.

Slinging the strap of her purse over her shoulder, she went to the door and stopped, staring at the glossily painted panels. The caterer had left a message for him at his office. There was nothing she could do about the mess. She should leave.

The situation would end up being blamed on her anyway, she argued with herself, her hand on the doorknob. So what did it matter if she left? Did she have to be here to suffer in person?

But rather than turn the knob and open the door, she stood dithering with herself, unable to abandon him. There had been something in his voice when he talked about this promotion, an emotional intensity unusual for him. She couldn't forget it.

Katie took her hand off the doorknob and paced several steps toward the living area before turning back toward the door. Normally Josh was so matter-of-fact, so irritatingly rational, but she'd heard longing in his voice when he talked about this job. Need.

Katie stopped pacing.

Without a doubt, Josh would blame her for whatever went wrong. His career-boosting, high-octane cocktail party would be a flaming failure. Yet another one laid at her door. No matter what she did, he'd be upset with her. But something inside her still couldn't abandon him to his crisis. She knew what it was like to be let down by others.

Regardless of whether or not the caterers had bailed on them, Josh was depending on her to help make this evening work. She might not completely understand why it was so important to him, but she knew it was. No matter how much she wanted to leave, to turn her back, she couldn't. Josh was counting on her—actually relying on her, for a change—and for some reason, that mattered.

Fifty people and no food. What the heck could she do?

She should call him, she thought, turning toward the phone she'd seen on the kitchen wall. After all, this was his shindig. He should at least help her decide how to deal with the crisis.

Katie frowned as she went into the spotless kitchen. She'd seen Josh at work, immersed to his eyebrows in whatever the heck he did in his corporate cell. It didn't take much imagination to envision his response to her phone call.

And what could he do from the office? It wasn't likely that he had a recipe for crab puffs in his head. She'd bet the man had never even made French toast.

Leaning back on the counter, Katie tossed her purse aside. She had to handle this herself and, in order to do that, she needed to think of something really fast.

"What do you mean, the caterers canceled?" Josh thundered, standing in the kitchen doorway four hours later.

"Some woman called and said they had screwed up and not written you down on the schedule," Katie said, glancing into the extra-large oven to see the pizza rolls crisping nicely.

"Katie!" he said imperatively. "Why didn't you call and tell me?"

She looked over her shoulder at him. "Norton's said she'd left a message at your office."

"Just a name and a number, nothing more! I didn't get a chance to call her back. I thought they were just phoning to confirm."

"I didn't know, but there wasn't anything you could have done about it from the office, anyway." She wiped her damp hands on a dish towel she'd found in a drawer. Ripping open a bag of prepared salad—at least that's what the bag said; to her it looked like a tangled clump of weeds—she dumped it out into a large bowl.

"So they told you they weren't coming and you didn't think we needed to talk about this?" he demanded, his voice rising in a very un-Josh-like way.

"It was already after lunch when she called," Katie said, arranging the chichi greens on a platter she'd borrowed from Bethany's mom. "I didn't really have time to track you down since I had to do something fast about the food."

"If you had called me," he said, throwing his keys on the counter in obvious exasperation, "I could have canceled the damn party!"

"No need!" she announced triumphantly as she took the tray of sizzling pizza rolls out of the oven and dropped the heap of them on a serving tray. "Voila! We have finger food."

Josh frowned down at the food, glancing for the first time at the fancied-up trays of dip and other nibblies she'd scrounged from the frozen section of the nearest grocery store.

"I can see you've gone to a lot of trouble," he said uneasily, "but I'm not sure—"

Picking up a pizza roll, Katie blew on it to cool it down and handed the crispy morsel to Josh. "Try."

"I just don't think—"

"Just try it," she admonished, pushing his hand toward his mouth.

"Okay," he mumbled around the still-warm tidbit. "Mmm. Not bad."

"Told you so," she said smugly, going to take a thawed container of jalapeño poppers out of the microwave.

Josh swallowed. "That was good, but, Katie, this group of people are accustomed to—"

"Big money food," she finished in a gently scoffing tone. "And they've seen it, eaten it a dozen times before. You're about to set a new trend."

"I am?" His one eyebrow climbed doubtfully higher.

"Yes," she said complacently. "We're serving your corporate drones with illicit pleasures."

"Excuse me?"

"Yes," she said, smirking with the joy of her own brilliance. "These people are busy, right? They spend all their time at work?"

"Most of them," he agreed reluctantly.

"So they eat convenience foods. Most of them probably go home after nine every night and nuke some sort of treat from the freezer. After a while of doing that, you get to like the freezer stuff. You know, the packaged stuff that's full of calories and fat? Lots of salt? Well, that's what we're giving them tonight. These are the things they love to eat, but never admit to touching."

"Like a theme party?" he said, still frowning, but the panicked note had left his voice.

"Yes," Katie said happily. "Now go get the drinks ready because they'll be here any minute."

Forty-five minutes later, she walked through the chattering crowd with a platter of goodies. Josh's party was off to a great start.

Across the room, he stood, his dark-gray suit jacket falling open as he leaned an arm against the mantel. But the look in his eyes belied his casual stance. She could see the sheer determination there, the hint of steel around his mouth as he stood talking to his boss, Dave Williams.

This was business for Josh, she realized. Deadly serious business. He stood holding a drink in his hand, smiling and interacting with the small group, but he wasn't having fun. Katie would have bet on it.

And their guests had only arrived a short time ago.

Conscious again of the determination to make this party work for him, she placed the platter of food on the serving table against one wall.

Once she'd gotten over her initial panic about the food, the cocktail party hadn't held much anxiety for her. She crossed the room again, smugly aware of how perfect her olive silk pantsuit was for this occasion. Sleeveless with a cropped top that fell just below her waist, the suit was both dressy, classic and flattering. The slim pants made the most of her legs—one of her best features, she thought, smirking—and she wasn't wearing black.

Though many of the other women in the room were. In the group chatting with the boss, a beautifully fair Madison stood wearing a slender black dress with pearls. She was smiling at some remark Josh had made, her lovely face serene except for the occasional flashes of embarrassment when her husband made a tacky comment.

Something Dave Williams was all too inclined to do.

Going back into the no-longer-spotless kitchen for another platter, Katie glanced as the door opened behind her.

Josh came into the room frowning. "I think this is everyone. The booze will hold out for a while. Do we have enough food?"

Lifting the platter in her hand, she said, "Not to worry. I bought enough for a buffalo herd."

"Thank God. At least no one's complaining about the hors d'oevres." He shoved a hand through his short, dark hair. "This chitchat crap will probably go on for another two hours or so. Then we can send them home."

He was worried. Despite the annoyance in his beautiful blue eyes and the tightness in his voice, Katie knew he was anxious.

After what he'd said the day they were shopping for clothes, she knew what this meant to him. Affluence. Always being able to take care of himself and his own.

Balancing the tray on one hand, Katie put the other on

his arm. "It's fine. Really. Go on in and enjoy your friends."

Josh scanned her face. Are you doing okay? I mean, everything is under control in here, but . . . are you comfortable with this crowd?"

"Of course. They're no different from any other bunch of hungry, overworked people."

"No one has said anything tacky or mean to you?" His gaze was unusually intent.

"Everyone has been wonderful," she said soothingly. He was worried about her? About how his coworkers and their spouses were treating her?

Katie couldn't help the warmth that flooded through her. Shifting her hand under the tray, she sent him a brilliant smile as a reward.

He looked down at her for a moment, an oddly struck expression on his face. "I'm glad you're here."

Katie looked up at him, a sudden prickling in her throat. "Me too. Now go on. Go have fun."

"That's not likely," he said under his breath as he turned toward the door in response to her urging. "Don't stay in here all night. Remember, you're my asset. Come mingle."

"I will." Following him into the crowded living area, she tried to ignore the sudden constricting in her heart. He'd looked so lost just now, with something of a little boy wistfulness on his face. He could be so darn sweet sometimes, so thoughtful. Those flashes of sensitivity kept jarring all her old opinions of him.

Seven

"Katie!" Madison called her as she slipped into the living room. Standing beside a walnut grandmother clock, a plate in her hand, the other woman said, "What a great idea for party food!"

A tall, blond man standing beside the serving table nodded, swallowing before saying, "Wonderful. Just like mother makes."

"Hey, Kirk," a woman wearing a business suit said, "your mother must have been Sara Lee."

A ripple of laughter ran through the group beside the table.

"Usually we get smoked salmon and shrimp mousse," Madison said, making a face even as she kept her voice low. "It's good, but it's always the same. This"—she pointed to the tray of jalapeño poppers—"is different!"

"I'm glad you like it." Katie took an empty tray off the table, replacing it with another.

"I do like it," Madison affirmed, "but I would expect the unexpected from you. You're so creative!"

"That's right," an older woman joined the group. "You're the photographer who's doing the club photos."

"I am," Katie confirmed as Dave Williams appeared

beside her, taking the last remaining tidbit from the tray she held.

"Good food," he said. "Makes a nice change."

"Thanks."

"Hey, Josh," Dave called out, still chewing the mouthful, "you should marry this woman. She really knows how to feed a hungry man."

From across the room, Josh's attention was distracted from the conversation he'd been holding with several others. He smiled at her. "Yes, she does."

Williams put his arm around Katie and squeezed her shoulder. "He's a lucky dog. You make sure he never forgets that."

"I will," she assured him, slipping out of the older man's embrace as gracefully as possible with the murmured excuse of taking the tray back to the kitchen.

As the evening wore on, the groups clustered in the earth-toned living area grew louder. Katie fancied they let go of their wolfish business personas under the influence of good food and drink and were now just having a good time.

The gathering was really low maintenance. Other than replacing the food trays every so often, Katie had little to do but meet and talk with Josh's chattering guests.

To her immense satisfaction, several women complimented her outfit—one of them in a surprised tone of voice. Katie smiled and accepted the praise, remembering well the other woman's mean-spirited remark at the banquet. Apparently, olive silk didn't bring out the same viciousness earned by gold sequins.

The men didn't comment on her outfit, but twice,

within Josh's hearing, she was told by one of his coworkers how lucky he was.

Katie beamed. She was wrapped in the feeling of being the highlight of the evening, and a happy little buzz zipped through her veins. For a night that had started from such a dismal beginning, things were going extremely well.

Once again, Josh's demands ended up bringing out the best in her, she thought as she brought a fresh drink to Rick Goring. What with the photography studio's growing success and her role in Josh's corporate world, she felt for the first time the hint of success. Real, earned success, not just something she'd pulled out of the fire in a haphazard way.

Aware of Josh's gaze following her several times as the evening wore on, she felt a surge of warmth. He'd relied on her to make this party happen for him and she'd pulled it off.

Across the room, masculine laughter rang out, drawing attention. Josh stood in a group with several people, all of whom were laughing at some joke. Pausing, she watched him, noting the relaxed set of his shoulders, the easy amusement on his face.

He was loosening up and as there was no glass in his hands, she felt safe in taking credit for his lessened tension. The party was going incredibly well. That had to be a relief to him. Katie smiled, turning back to the woman she'd been chatting with.

Whether he knew it or not, she was having a good effect on Josh, too.

"Katie," Madison appeared next to her. "How are the portraits going?"

"Very well. I had sittings all week. Aren't you sched-uled this next week?"

"Yes." Madison flushed. "Dave wants—"

"There's my little wifey." Her husband came over and slung his arm around her shoulders. Although he'd been drinking steadily all evening and his eyes were bright, he didn't seem unsteady on his feet or slur his words. "Did she tell you what we want?"

"Not yet," his wife said, smoothing her black dress with a nervous smile.

Dave lowered his voice, leaning toward Katie in an exaggerated manner. "Do you do nudes? She's a little shy, but I'd like a nude of my little Maddy."

Katie's gaze ricocheted off his florid countenance to his wife's still-flushed face. She couldn't help but feel a pang of sympathy for the woman. However, at least her husband hadn't yelled the request so everyone could hear. Appar-ently, he did have some sensitivity.

Sending the other woman a reassuring smile, Katie said, "I'm sure we can do some portraits you'll both like."

She glanced up then, her gaze colliding with Josh's as he came across the room to where she stood.

Casually sliding his arm around her, Josh made some comment to Rick who stood chatting to their boss.

It was as if a light had been turned on in her body, Katie thought in startled realization. Just his resting his arm around her, the warmth of him close beside her, left her body clamoring with awareness. The strength in his body—which she remembered so well from the two em-braces they'd shared—set off a thrumming in her heart. Through the texture of his suit coat and stiff white shirt, she felt his lithe power, the unconscious sexiness he exuded.

". . . really handled that situation with Wellsat," Rick said to his boss, his easy admiration in his words and on his face. "They know they can't jack us around now."

Dave laughed. "Yes. I called Tucker and made some noise.

Rick sent Josh a flash of a sly smile before saying to his boss, "Yes, sir. Sometimes that's what it takes."

Josh stood silently beside her, listening to their conversation, his arm still curved around her shoulder. She felt the brush of his gaze along the curve of her face.

". . . have to handle that yourself next time," Dave Williams was saying. "Is the Op-Com situation going well now that we've got the contracts signed?"

"Very well," Josh answered, his voice quietly confident.

"Good." Williams took another sip of his drink. "Of course, that deal means millions to the company."

"Yes."

Glancing up, Katie recognized the carefulness in Josh's eyes, a kind of watchful awareness that had even been there earlier when he'd laughed with his friends. Nothing about his demeanor around his boss suggested the easy manipulativeness she saw in Rick. Instead, Josh seemed to play his hand carefully, apparently always respectful. But always careful, also.

The conversation ebbed and flowed around them and Katie stayed beside him, not wanting to leave the warmth at his side, not wanting to leave him alone to do battle.

Because that's what he seemed to be doing. A very

civilized form of feint and parry, a very conscious playing of the corporate politics that seemed so foreign to her.

Now that she thought about it, how often had she ever seen Josh without that conscious carefulness in his eyes? He was surrounded here by people who relied on him every day, people who benefitted from the good work he did. But apparently he didn't feel safe.

Never safe. Never able to trust.

With a stab of regret, Katie thought about her sister. Maybe Josh had reason to doubt the goodwill of those around him. After all, he'd been betrayed not only by a woman he'd selflessly offered to help, but by his only brother, as well.

Erin had never cared for him, Katie thought with sudden certainty. Not really. *Not like I do.* Did Erin ever understand what drove Josh? Ever know the things that were important to him?

Her sister hadn't thought it necessary. To her, he'd been an answer to a dilemma that had eventually resolved itself and made Josh expendable. Still, the thought that he'd been engaged to her sister nagged at Katie. It hadn't been an engagement based on emotion, but the man had been involved with her sister. Shouldn't that make him off limits?

Looking at him now as he talked so seriously with his coworkers, Katie knew he needed a woman who could understand. Who would tease him into playing when he needed to relax. A woman to shout at him when he was too full of his own agenda.

He needed her.

And Katie needed him. Needed his belief in her. Needed to be in his arms.

* * *

Two hours later, Josh shut the door on the last of his lingering guests. His head pounded, not from the three sips he'd taken of the drink he'd been nursing all evening, but from the effort it took to play the game.

He'd never be as good at it as Rick was, but he'd long accepted the pseudosocial aspect of success in the corporate world. And the evening had gone surprisingly well.

Because of Katie.

To his shock, she'd pulled off her weird party menu with style—the same style with which she wore the green pants outfit he hadn't wanted to buy for her. The same way she'd laughingly handled his boss and his coworkers. She had social skills, without a doubt.

Tonight, she'd managed to fit into his business gathering while still looking both exotic and sexy as hell. She was both charming and playfully respectful toward the man who held his promotion hostage.

"Are they gone?" she called out, coming through the swinging door from the kitchen.

"Yes." He took off his suit coat and slung it over the back of a chair.

"Don't you think it went really well?" she asked, a glowing enthusiasm on her face.

"Yes," he said with relief. "Yes. It went really well. You did a good job."

She shrugged happily. "It wasn't so hard. Like any other group, if you feed and water them, they're happy."

Josh sank onto the couch, rolling his shoulders to release tension. "I need them to be happy."

Her gaze rested on him for a moment before she put

down the glass she'd picked up from a table. She crossed the living room and came to stand behind where he sat on the couch.

"You're entirely too good at this to be so tense," she said, her hands suddenly on his shoulders, her fingers massaging his muscles. "Relax."

Josh went still, tensing further at her touch. Not from any work-related concern, but because the stroke of her fingers on his shoulders brought an instantaneous response to his body.

Incredibly aware of the warmth of her hands on him through the cotton of his shirt, he consciously leaned into her touch. All evening, his awareness of Katie had intruded on his concentration. Her light, silvery laughter had threaded through every conversation. The scent of her had teased his nose when he'd drawn her close in a demonstration of their supposed intimacy.

It was a familiarity he wanted to make very real, he knew as he breathed in her fragrance now. Ever since he'd seen her lying like a delectable morsel on that satin bed, ever since he'd kissed her again, he'd spent way too much time fantasizing about making love to Katie.

Kissing her hot, hungry mouth, covering her slender curvaceous body with his own. She made him hot, left him dizzy with wanting. Every time she came within five feet of him, she just about drove him over the edge of his self-control.

"Josh," she said softly, her hands sliding forward over his chest, her voice at his ear.

He turned his head, his gaze tangling with hers. So near, so velvety green.

"Josh, make love to me."

He blinked, distrusting his ears. Had she actually *asked* him to make love to her? It didn't seem possible that their minds and bodies were united with such a similarly urgent need.

But he couldn't doubt the glowing invitation in her eyes or question the message when she leaned forward, pressing her mouth against his neck.

It only took one tiny flick of her hot tongue against his skin to galvanize him out of his stunned state.

Reaching around, Josh slid a hand down to her stomach as Katie bent forward over the back of the couch. With his other hand bracing her shoulder, he half-lifted her over the couch. She tumbled forward and fell onto the couch, her head landing in his lap.

He looked down at her, his heart slamming against his rib cage. She was there in his lap, her red-gold hair framing her flushed face, her moist lips parted, a feast of erotic possibilities. With his hand beneath her neck, he lifted her mouth to his own, greedily kissing her, his body hardening instantaneously.

Meeting his hunger with her own, she clung to him, lifting her mouth to his, her tongue eager. He held her, pillaging her mouth beneath his, his hand beneath the green top she wore. There he found her breasts and covered one smooth, heated mound with his hand, kneading her and plucking at her taut nipple through the silken cover of her bra.

Her breath tangled on a soft sob of arousal as he lifted his lips from hers. Drawing her closer, he sought the sweet hollow of her neck, while he fumbled for the buttons at the back of her top.

He needed her to be naked. Needed her breasts free to

his touch, needed her sprawled across his legs all bare and flushed and begging for his touch. His head pounded now with another kind of pain, a driving, piercing urgency to take her. To lave and suckle every inch of her, every delicate curve, every rounded morsel.

"Damn!" he muttered beneath his breath, fighting the tangle of green fabric, the thwarting resistance of buttons he couldn't see.

She lay half turned toward him on his lap, her head thrown back, the tangle of her red silken hair sprawling across his knees. Blue eyes wide open, her breath coming in small pants between her bruised berry lips, she moaned an urgent little sound that nearly sent him over the edge.

Lifting her with a jerk, Josh slid both hands beneath her back to conquer the recalcitrant fasteners. He dipped his head, tracing the shell of her ear with his tongue, tugging at her earlobe with his teeth.

Katie sobbed, her body moving against his with an echoing urgency.

Never again, he swore to himself, would he buy her clothes that buttoned up the back! Better yet, he'd keep her naked, her full breasts free and available to his whims, her long, succulent legs free for his caressing hands. They'd both live that way, naked and accessible twenty-four hours a day. He couldn't imagine ever tiring of this heady rush, this conquering need to mate with her.

At last! The final button pulled free and Josh jerked at her top, slowing only to thread her arms free. She lay back across his lap then, her shoulders and stomach gleaming pearl-white. Still determined to be free of any impediment, he found the clasp of her bra and tore it loose.

Her breasts filled his hands, each rose-tipped peak begging for his mouth. Bending down, he licked and kissed her, drawing one puckered nipple into his mouth while he plucked the other with restless fingers.

Dimly, he felt her yanking at his tie, realized she was doing her own battle with the buttons of his shirt.

He himself had too much fascination with the hollow of her bare shoulder, the valley between her breasts. He was no help to her. By the time he'd discovered the flavor of her ivory skin where it curved gently over the crest of her collarbone, she'd opened his shirt all the way and slid her hand over his chest.

His skin felt on fire beneath her stroking touch, like the trail of fire beneath a striking match. She slid her hands over him, brushing her palms along his rib cage, lingering in her exploration. Cool and slender, her hand pressed against the thunder of his heart.

With one hand tugging at her turgid nipple, Josh groped for the zipper at the back of her slacks. It slid down, demure and cooperative, and he slipped his hand into her pants, cupping the warm curves of her fanny as she lay across his lap facing him.

Beautiful, pliant and hot. He stroked her, his fingers flexing over her silken textures.

His face buried in the hollow of her neck, his hands full of naked Katie, he wasn't at first aware of her pulling away.

"Just a minute," she whispered, her husky voice sending a thrill through him.

Josh straightened, staring into her face with a dazed abstraction. Sitting up, she stood in front of the couch, her upper torso bare, her succulent breasts tempting as sin. But as he watched, she slipped the green pants and her panties down, lower and lower, till the dark red thatch between her legs became visible. He reached for her then, not caring that she hadn't completely freed her legs of the tangling pants.

But she held him off with a restraining hand pressed to the wall of his bare chest. He'd hardly been aware of rising to stand next to her, but she tugged his shirt off his shoulders and loosened his trousers till they fell around his ankles.

If she'd been slow about it, he'd have had to protest. But Katie disrobed him with every evidence of the same urgency clawing at him. She only paused briefly to stroke his arousal through the thin cotton knit of his briefs.

Josh closed his eyes, controlling the urge to flinch from the bolt of pleasure. Just her hand gliding over him threatened his control and when she turned into his arms and pressed her mouth and damp tongue against his torso, he couldn't contain himself any longer.

Whipping off his shorts, he pressed her down on the couch, spreading her legs so he could kneel before her on the cushioned surface. With one slender calf thrown over the back of the couch, she gave him access to her whole self.

God.

He paused, his dazed brain burning out circuits from the unbelievably beautiful sight before him. Katie completely naked, splayed like a sacrifice, her wanton eyes clinging to his own nakedness, her hands urging him forward.

He wanted this to be so good for her.

In that piercing moment, he ruthlessly pushed back his

own burgeoning arousal and bent to touch his tongue to the sweet fiery glory between her legs.

She shrieked, the small sound, desperately erotic as she bucked under his touch.

Filling his hands with her slender buttocks, he teased at her hot core, loving the gasping sobs his ministrations drew from her. Slick and responsive, she heated for him like butter in the sun.

"Please, please, please," she cried breathlessly moments later. "I want it! Now!"

Not lifting his mouth from her thrashing body, Josh groped for his trousers on the floor next to the couch. There in his wallet was tucked one condom, so beautifully within reach.

Straightening, he sheathed himself in the latex as swiftly as possible and bent to enter her with one hard stroke.

Katie enclosed him, her flesh welcoming and clinging, stroking, yielding, calling him back, over and over. He felt the clench of her muscles, heard the catching of her breath in her throat. Soft, panting moans came through her parted lips.

"Oh, God. Oh, God."

As her body tightened around his own burning flesh, he felt his control splintering, felt the shattering of his head, his soul, his whole body tightening in a rush of incredible pleasure. Endless, endless. More than he'd ever known.

She was glorious beneath him. Hot and wet. Incredibly responsive.

Thrusting into her wildly, he heard her gasp out, heard

her cry out again, and then the driving rhythm blocked everything but the splintering, jagged pleasure.

Seconds, eons later, he fell against her, exhausted, only conscious enough to brace his full weight from her slender frame.

After a few minutes, the thundering in his ears faded some and he heard her whisper.

"I can die now," she said, the words thready and faint. "I've already seen heaven."

With the faint light of dawn calling her, Katie rolled over in the big king-sized bed, snuggling against Josh's back with a complete sense of contentment. His skin felt beautiful beneath the slide of her palm, warm and firm and alive. She wanted to memorize the feel of him—the muscled contours of his back, the powerful sweep of his shoulders.

"It's really hard to sleep with a hot, insatiable woman running her hands over you," he growled, rolling over to gather her into his arms.

Katie burrowed closer, loving the cuddling of her nakedness against his. Despite the late, eventful night, she felt vibrantly alive as the sun crept over the windowsill.

"I'm not the only insatiable one," she reminded him. After they'd come together in that first explosion of passion on the couch, he'd carried her tenderly to his bed and made love to her until she'd sobbed his name over and over in mindless release.

"No," he agreed, glancing over his shoulder at the clock on the bedside table. "Almost time to get up."

"Mmmm." She pressed a small kiss against his shoulder, thinking of his going to work and getting on with the battle. Did he ever give himself a moment's rest? A moment when he didn't have to plow forward toward that ever-present goal?

"If I'd known I had this consolation to look forward to," he said, drawing his hand over her bare hip, "I wouldn't have worried so much about the cocktail party going well."

"It did go well, didn't it?" she said smugly. He'd relied on her and she'd pulled it off.

"Yes," Josh said, bending forward to kiss her before getting out of the bed. "Who would have ever thought *you* could make food for fifty people?"

Katie stared after him as he disappeared into the bathroom.

"I thought I was screwed for sure when I saw that crazy stuff you were serving," he said, his voice echoing off the bathroom tiles.

"You did?" She tried to ignore the faint sinking feeling in her stomach.

"Of course," he said with a chuckle that grated on her. "I mean, who would think people who are used to the very best caterers would get a kick out of the frozen appetizers and TV food you gave them."

"*I* thought they would," she said, trying to push aside the flickering irritation at the casual contempt she heard in his voice. "And they certainly ate enough."

"They were starved," Josh said dismissively, his oblivious amusement floating through the open bathroom door along with the sounds of the shower being turned on. "We were just lucky they thought it was cool party food in a hip, oddball kind of way."

"Yes, they did," she said, her disquiet bringing her upright in the bed.

"Next time," he said, briefly sticking his head around the door, "next time, I make sure the caterer has been confirmed. We don't want to run that kind of risk again. This time it worked out, but I'm not counting on your Flanagan luck."

He saw it as a fluke, Katie realized with a sinking feeling of nausea in her middle. Her fabulous, creative moment of success, and Josh thought of it as random good fortune.

Not an achievement on her part, nothing she'd actually done. Just luck! She was just another flighty, unreliable, *lucky* Flanagan.

She crawled out of his bed, the thoughts in her head as tangled as the sheets they'd shared. Had Josh really had any faith in her ability to handle the party last night? At all? Or had he accepted her hastily prepared hors d'oevres because he had no other options?

"You know," she said, an edge in her voice, "I worked really hard to make that party come together last night."

The shower still running, he came to stand in the doorway, an annoying grin on his face. "Yeah, opening all those boxes of frozen food."

"You jerk!" she sputtered, suddenly irate. "I'd like to have seen you put together food for fifty people in so short a time."

Josh shrugged. "Come on, Katie. Don't make such a big deal of it. The crowd from work was hungry and thought your stuff was a cute idea. It's not like rocket science to nuke some snack foods."

She gasped. "Of all the arrogant, self-absorbed asses,

you're the worst! I could have walked out and left you with no food for your crowd!"

"Or you could have called me," he shot back, as angry now as she was. "I would have gotten hold of everyone and canceled the evening."

"Oh!" Katie shrieked in frustration, charging out of his bedroom and down the short hall to gather up her scattered clothes from the area around the couch.

Josh followed her, a towel knotted around his waist. "Why are you making such a big deal of this? The party went well. They liked the food and we had a really wonderful evening together."

Holding her clothes in front of her nakedness like a shield, Katie stalked past him and went into the spare room to dress.

"Listen," he said from the doorway, "I have to get ready for work. We can talk about this later."

Scrambling into her things, her back to the door, Katie blinked back the tears in her eyes. "There's nothing for us to talk about."

She knew he hesitated in the doorway a moment before going back into his room. The door to the shower opened and closed.

Dragging her shirt on, she muttered a curse at him under her breath. How could she have been so stupid? What she'd seen last night as his belief in her ingenuity had actually been resignation. As soon as he'd realized the caterers weren't coming, he'd clearly written the party off as a failure.

Here she'd been worrying about him these past few days, aware of what drove him toward success, concerned that he did his battling alone. And all the while, he'd thought of her only as that Flanagan mess. A girl too often engaged and too frequently seeking escape from the trials of life.

She *had* tried to escape too often, she admitted bitterly to herself. Her foolish sentimentality had led her to leap before she looked. She'd found herself in jobs and relationships that simply weren't right. And here she was, in a mess again. Too quick to throw herself into caring, too heedless of her own heart.

But this time she hadn't fallen into infatuation with his looks, hadn't jumped into a commitment because he seemed so likeable. This time, she'd looked at a man and seen his fears, seen the uncertainties behind his confidence, the need he felt for assurances he'd never had.

She'd seen his heart and lost her own. This time she'd fallen in love with a man who could barely see her for the phantoms of his own childhood.

Wiping in disgust at the dampness on her cheek, Katie went quickly into the living room.

She'd been loving him, supporting him, giving her all to his cause and he was so consumed with the career path before him that he couldn't get beyond his preconceived Flanagan notions.

"So," Rick said with an exaggerated lift of his eyebrow, "I hear you had lunch with Dave?"

"Yes." Pushing at the rolled-back cuff of his shirt sleeve, Josh checked the time. "We had lunch. No big deal. He wanted to go over several projects on my desk."

Rick propped himself on the edge of Josh's desk. "Of course, he did. But he didn't have to foot the bill for lunch if he didn't want to. You're in! That fabulous cocktail party worked! I told you the bimbo would do it."

"She's not a bimbo," Josh snapped.

"Maybe not," his friend said, obviously unrepentant, "but she's got all the right qualifications. I'd say with her on your arm, you've jumped ahead of the rest and you're on the fast track for that promotion. You're playing the game and it's paying off!"

"Nothing's guaranteed," Josh told him, suppressing a surge of annoyance. Usually Rick's irreverent, amoral approach to corporate politics amused him, but lately his own frustration with the game-playing had left him irritated and short-tempered.

He'd been wondering lately just how much of his soul he'd have to sell to reach the pinnacle in his career.

"No, the promotion isn't guaranteed," Rick agreed, "but you have to admit you're a much more likely candidate for that promotion. Listen, I've got that meeting. I'll see you later."

"Yeah." He raised a hand in farewell as his friend left.

Despite the faint distaste he'd been conscious of the last few weeks, he did realize he was making strides in the right direction. Dave Williams asked his opinion about ticklish dilemmas, included him in on developing plans and asked him to play golf.

All because the SOB now thought Josh was like him. It was a sobering, not altogether heartening thought.

Who would have thought fickle Katie Flanagan would be such an asset to him? In the two days since their cocktail party, Dave had mentioned the gathering three times. Along with the rest of the office crew, he'd been enchanted by Katie's casual style of entertaining and her beauty.

Josh, on the other hand, couldn't stop thinking of her lips, her long legs wrapped around him; the soft natural scent he'd discovered in the cleft between her breasts.

How good he'd felt with her wrapped all around him. He'd made love to her and felt like he was on top of the world. What man didn't fantasize about a beautiful woman like Katie coming apart in his arms? Sobbing his name in ecstasy and begging him to make love to her again.

Damn.

And now she was furious with him.

Josh got up, went to the window and looked out unseeing at the Dallas skyline.

Being with Katie had made him feel invincible. Not just the lovemaking, although it had been the most incredible experience of his life, but afterwards, the tender sense of connection. The soft, shared laughter in the dark.

It left him feeling strange in a really terrific way. Left him wanting to see her, to hear her voice.

She'd been really upset when she'd left his apartment. He wasn't even sure exactly why, but he kept thinking about it, wondering how the morning had gone so wrong.

It was just sex between them, he'd told himself again and again. But that squishy soft feeling in his gut when he thought of her, that wasn't about sex. The way he'd hear a phrase and think of her.

They had a business deal. If they'd found each other attractive enough to have phenomenally incredible sex, that didn't have to mean anything more than sex.

He'd gotten accustomed, as most men were, to being aroused by parts of women. Their breasts, legs or butt. It just seemed to come with the testosterone. He worked hard at treating his female coworkers equally and had made it a rule never to hit on someone he worked with.

But this thing with Katie left him feeling odd. Left him thinking about her, fighting with the urge to apologize, for what he wasn't sure. He wasn't sure he liked these emotions, really. But he couldn't say he disliked them, either.

Normally it would have been a relief to have a sex partner leave so conveniently the morning after. No fuss, no awkwardness. But Katie had left mad.

Leaving the window, he went back to sit at his desk, pulling the work toward him, trying without much success to focus his wandering thoughts.

Katie really had handled the cocktail party well, turning it from potential disaster to an unexpected triumph, all in the face of a complete lack of experience. It may have been the least likely kind of luck, but she hadn't known how well the thing would turn out. She really did have her own brand of bravery.

He shouldn't have been so dismissive when they talked about it that morning.

Josh dropped his pen onto the desk and stared unseeing ahead of him. Never in his life had he made love to such a woman, such a sexually responsive, alive creature.

She'd made *him* feel more strong, more brave, more everything. Made him mad for her and he couldn't forget, couldn't help wanting more.

The contract on his desk forgotten, he glanced at the phone and wondered what she was doing at that moment. Wondered if she'd welcome yet another apologetic telephone call.

Eight

"Erin!" Katie leaned back against the reception desk, the phone cradled to her ear, its cord twisted nervously in her hand. "I'm glad I caught up with you."

"Hey, little sister. What's shaking?" Erin said, sounding like she'd just woken up despite the fact that it was afternoon in her current time zone.

"I, uh, just called about the studio." The lie slipped out before Katie knew it. How could she say why she was calling her sister? *Hello, I just slept with a man you used to be engaged to, but never loved? He's a jackass and an idiot and I can't stop thinking about him.*

"The studio?" Erin echoed, the sound of a smothered yawn clear over the phone line.

"Granddaddy Flanagan's photography studio," Katie clarified, rubbing a hand over tired eyes. "Remember I talked to you a month ago about Josh foreclosing on it?"

"Oh, yeah. Too bad, but I guess he got tired of holding the note." Erin sounded vaguely regretful. "I kind of left that in his hands."

"Yes," Katie said, an unaccustomed dry tone to the word. "But I-I convinced him to let me have an extension. Six months to get it up and running before I start making payments."

"Really?" Interest flickered in Erin's voice. "What did you have to do? Sleep with him?"

Her sister's question, offered in such a casual manner, startled Katie into momentary silence.

"You did!" Erin concluded, sounding amused and completely untroubled. "Well, good for you. And for Josh."

"I didn't sleep with him so he'd give me a chance to reopen the studio!" Katie blurted out. "We made a different kind of deal."

"Did you?" A muffled noise from Erin's end of the conversation told Katie her sister wasn't alone. In a moment, Erin said, "Well, you know if you do sleep with him, it's nothing to me. I never slept with him. I've always felt kind of bad about Josh. He really did try to help me when I was panicked about being preggers."

"Yes, he did try to help," Katie agreed, thinking of Josh and his innate sense of honor. Josh and his inability to rely on another Flanagan. He thought her a flake and an incompetent. Josh had less belief in her than she did in herself.

"Did Mom tell you about the band?" Erin asked suddenly.

"Oh, yes."

Katie held the phone up to her ear, listening to her sister's recital of triumphs in a string of small clubs over the northwest. Even with her heart aching and her being furious with Josh, she still owed her sister a little interest.

"I'm glad things are going so well for you," she said finally, the weight of sisterly guilt lifted from her burdened conscious. She'd been a fool to get emotionally involved with Josh, but at least she hadn't betrayed Erin in the bargain.

"So, things are going good with the studio?"

"Yes," Katie answered, her thoughts of Josh all tangled up with regret and longing and anger. "I'm rounding up some new business."

"Great. Hey, I have to go." The mumbled conversation behind Erin intruded again. "But, listen, if you did sleep with Josh and you ever want to do it again, I say, go for it. That boy deserves some fun."

"Okay," Katie said slowly. Sleeping with Josh again was the last thing she needed to do.

"Maybe I should move to Kentucky. Or Australia," Katie mused, trying to keep the discouragement out of her voice.

Across the table outside the student union, her friend, Bethany, opened a sandwich and took a bite. Lunch was spread between them, a collection of plastic-wrapped food items gathered from the lunchroom inside.

The late spring sun was warm on Katie's back, but she felt strangely cold despite that fact. She'd felt angry and lost all morning, coming to have lunch with Bethany at school as a way of escaping her own thoughts.

"You want to move to Australia because of Josh?" Bethany asked after chewing for a moment.

Katie worked at the clingy plastic encasing her boiled egg, using the exercise to avoid answering immediately. While her fingers were busy, she mentally wrestled to free herself of the fog of disappointment and anger that had surrounded her since she'd left Josh's apartment the day before.

He'd never really believed in her. Never thought she

was useful or capable of more than being a transient bed partner.

A bee hummed past her ear, apparently intent on the flowering vine just beyond their table.

"He's a jerk and this deal of ours just isn't working out," she said finally, making the words firm.

"Hmm," Bethany bit off another piece of sandwich. "Let's see. You just told me you had four sittings yesterday and three more this afternoon. So what's not working?"

"Money isn't everything," Katie said loftily, still working at getting the damned egg free.

"No, but it's something," her friend said in a dry voice. "And what's more, it's something neither you nor I have much of."

Katie gave up on the egg, which had apparently been glued into the plastic wrap, and turned her attention to a bowl of uninspiring fruit salad. "That may be true, but we're both still perfectly happy with our lives."

The lie tasted sour on her tongue.

Bethany's sardonic gaze swung up from the remains of her sandwich.

"You're going to be a surgeon one day," Katie told her, "and I'm going to be a world-famous photographer."

"Okay." The other woman picked up a paper napkin and dusted her fingers.

"I could move to Colorado," Katie said a moment later, trying to ignore the hint of desperation in her own voice. "Or Seattle. I hear they're both wonderful places to live."

"That's what I've heard," Bethany agreed, but the skepticism in her dark eyes didn't change.

"I could travel," Katie went on stubbornly, still listing her options. "See the world. I don't have to be stuck here in one place, taking pictures of people all the time. I could be a photojournalist and go wandering the countryside, capturing the natural environment."

"I thought you liked taking pictures of people," her friend pointed out as she polished an apple with another napkin.

Katie paused, remembering Camille's shy smile. She thought of the young mother and baby she'd worked with the day before. In one particular shot, she'd actually captured the budding likeness in their smiles.

She *did* like working with people.

"I can have more than one talent, can't I?" she demanded, pushing aside the fruit salad.

"Yes. You can have as many as you like," Bethany said graciously.

"Thank you." Katie smiled at her friend, the coldness in her middle easing some.

"But I think this is all about Josh," Bethany declared, taking a bite of apple.

Katie looked at her, furiously trying to suppress the quivering sensation that rose instantly in her chest. *She didn't love him. Didn't.* She'd been wrong about that.

No matter how much he disturbed her and set her body ablaze. No matter how much she wanted to make him see that not getting his promotion wouldn't be the end of the world, it wasn't that she loved him.

She'd been wrong about that, she told herself again. Pity was what she felt for Josh. Pity and disgust and fury. He was arrogant and unappreciative and he deserved her to leave him high and dry.

"No," she said abruptly, "it's not about him. Maybe I was confused about the studio. Maybe it was all just sentimental stuff about my grandfather and my childhood. I think what I really need is to expand my world and travel a lot."

Taking another bite of apple, Bethany shot her a long look, before agreeing, "Travel can be good."

"Yes." Katie leaned back against the cool metal chair. "It will be great to see the world. Taking photographs and bringing the world's beauty to others who don't have the options to go see it themselves."

"True."

"Bali. The Great Barrier Reef. That wall in China."

"Your red hair ought to go over big in the Orient," Bethany said with a laugh. "It's true that there are many wonderful places to see."

"Yes." Katie's voice wavered, her flash of bravado having burned itself out. She was angry and sad and completely miserable.

"If you could get to New York, one of the big news magazines, you could find work easily," Bethany declared. "Show them your portfolio. That will impress them."

"But I don't know anyone in New York." Her protest sounded weak to her own ears and, to her disgust, she suddenly felt like bursting out crying.

Bethany waved her hand dismissively. "I know someone. He's in the magazine business, too."

"You do?" Battling the urge to sniff, Katie forced a smile.

"My friend, Jerry. He's big in advertising, works with all the major rags or whatever they call them."

"I don't have a college degree," Katie reminded her in a small voice.

"Doesn't matter," Bethany said. "Just show them your recent work and they'll know you have the technical know-how. You might have to start small and work your way up. You know, be a flunky and run errands for a few years, but that wouldn't be so bad."

"No." Katie tried not to make the word sound too doubtful. If she didn't mind working like a slave to make the studio successful, why should going to New York and working hard sound so unappealing?

"Shall I call Jerry tonight?" Bethany asked. "You could be on a plane tomorrow."

Katie thought of Josh, remembering his face that day in the department store dressing room when he'd talked about them both being on display. She'd seen a worn-down kind of vulnerability in his eyes behind the tough-guy expression. A man who'd been fighting battles too long on his own and couldn't admit to needing help. Couldn't accept any vulnerability in himself.

Maybe that was why he'd been such a jerk about the party, so unable to acknowledge her contributions to its success. Of course, his reasons for needing the promotion didn't excuse his behavior after they had made love all night.

"Tomorrow?" Katie echoed a moment later. "I have Madison scheduled for a sitting tomorrow.

Bethany shrugged. "If you're not trying to make a go of the studio, who cares?"

"I care," Katie shot back. "I mean, Madison's husband wants some boudoir photos and she's really nervous about doing them. I think she'd be more comfortable with me than with a stranger."

A ghost of a smile coasted across Bethany's face. It

disappeared so swiftly Katie thought she must have imagined the expression.

"Okay. Then you can't leave tomorrow."

Katie picked up a discarded wrapper from her lunch tray, crumpling the paper in nervous hands.

"I can tell Jerry you need a week to get there."

"I don't know, Beth," Katie said after a long moment. "Maybe I should think this thing out. Josh might be an arrogant, selfish idiot, but I made a commitment to hang in there with him until the promotion is decided."

"Yes, you did."

Katie looked down at the crumpled wad of paper in her hands. "My sister was really tacky in the way she broke up with him. Even she feels bad about it and the whole situation left Josh convinced Flanagans are unreliable. He already thinks I'm a huge flake. The biggest Flanagan screw-up ever. I can't confirm it for him by acting anything like Erin."

The only reason she was staying, and sacrificing a wonderful chance at a career in photojournalism, was that she needed to follow through on this. For herself. It had nothing to do with Josh.

"You don't want to act like Erin," Bethany agreed softly.

Katie didn't know why it was so important to disprove his assessment of all Flanagans. She couldn't change his opinion of her sister and didn't really want to. Erin had behaved badly back then, as she'd acknowledged.

But somehow, Katie was determined to change Josh Morgan's opinion of herself. If nothing else, she'd make him admit she wasn't a flake. No matter how tempting running off to New York sounded, she couldn't dump their deal, even if it had taken on some unexpected risks to herself.

"I'll stay here and help him till he gets his damned promotion," she said finally. "But I'm not sleeping with him."

Regardless of her sister's good wishes on that score.

Bethany's eyebrows raised in casual interest. "Was that part of the deal?"

"No!"

"Well, then, he can't demand or expect you to do anything you don't want to do," her friend said with a sly smile. "Of course, what you *want* to do is up to you."

"I'm not sleeping with him," Katie said less forcefully. His tender kisses replayed themselves automatically then, just the memory raising a shiver of pleasure in her. "No, I can't sleep with him."

"Okay." Bethany eyed her curiously from across the table.

Glancing down at the fingers she'd tangled together in her lap, Katie struggled to push away the swamp of emotion in her stomach. He'd made love to her like a dream come true. And afterward, he'd held her in the dark while they laughed about silly things.

What would it be like to live like that? To share every night, every day and all the things in one's life.

She'd made him laugh and Josh really needed to laugh more, she thought inconsequentially.

They'd made love all night long and he'd turned into a callous brute the next morning. Thinking about it made her want to hit him.

"Okay," Bethany said again. "Well, let me know if you want me to call my friend."

"I will." She'd stay for now, Katie decided. But she couldn't have casual sex with Josh, no matter what he expected. He was breathtakingly virile and demanding in ways that raised massive confusion in her. He was alone. And he had no idea how he tugged at her heart, how he made her furious and made her want to cry, all at the same time.

He thought she was loony and unreliable. But she wasn't going to give him the satisfaction of sending her running off to New York. She'd stay and make him eat his words.

"I'm glad you could arrange your schedule to be available to play golf today," Josh said after Katie locked the studio door and came to join him in his car.

Her smile was glittering bright, but held little warmth. "It's part of the deal we made. You give me a chance to get the studio going and I help you with your promotion endeavors. I'm just following through on our agreement."

"I-I tried to call you yesterday," he said, eyeing her uncertainly.

"I got your message on the machine," she said with a strangely neutral cheerfulness.

Katie wasn't usually a woman who easily hid her feelings, Josh thought. A guy never had to guess where he was with her. When she was happy, she was breathtakingly happy. Her anger was obviously just as apparent, despite the knife-sharp smile. He'd always liked her openness and now found himself floundering to get a read on her true feelings.

"I called because I wanted to apologize," he said, as he drove. "Again."

She glanced at him. "Okay."

"Getting this promotion has really been occupying my mental energy." He looked over at her. "I'm afraid I wasn't very good at showing my appreciation for your help the other night."

"Don't worry about it," she told him, that steely smile still on her face. "I haven't."

"I really do appreciate everything you did," he said, struggling on in the face of her anger. "I couldn't have pulled it off on my own."

"You could have just canceled it," she reminded him with an edge to her voice.

"I could," he said, "but even if I'd rescheduled, I don't think they'd have liked the catered food as much as yours."

She said nothing, the smile vanishing from her face.

"Am I forgiven?" he found himself asking softly.

She sent him an unreadable glance before saying quietly, "Yes, Josh. Of course you're forgiven."

Josh glanced down the fairway, looked down at the ball and swung.

"Not bad," Dave congratulated him as the ball arced through the air, dropping through the warm Texas air to bounce on the jewel-bright green.

"Thanks." Josh walked back to the golf cart, passing Katie and Madison where they stood chatting as he went to slide his club into his bag.

His pretend fiancée looked beautiful today, her tumble of red hair swept off her face, her blue eyes cool.

He was definitely *not* forgiven, no matter what she said.

Behind him, his boss swung. "Damn. That could have been better."

The older man watched his ball land before turning to Josh. "So what do you think the company needs to do to put the southwest division at the top of sales this year?"

"Madison!" Dave interrupted the conversation before Josh could answer to call to his wife. "Come on, honey. You're holding up play."

"Oh, I'm sorry." She went to her bag and selected a club.

Josh wiped his hands on the towel attached to his golf bag, trying to formulate the most effective response to Dave's question. Although they weren't in the office and were accompanied by their respective women, he'd have had to be an idiot not to know this golf outing was primarily business.

Rather than distressing him, however, this reality gave him something to sink his teeth into. He'd prefer substance anytime over the murkier waters of semisocial events and back-slapping old-boys clubs.

Glancing over to where Katie stood watching, Josh thought again about his apology and the shadows he'd seen in her eyes. They bothered him more than her anger. Despite the fact that she'd voiced her forgiveness, he still saw that unusual reserve in her expression, the way she shifted away from his touch. He really had been a jerk that morning, he acknowledged.

Reacting instinctively to the disturbing intimacy growing between them, it had almost been as if he were trying to remind himself who she was . . . and who she was related to. And all the reasons why he shouldn't let himself care for her.

Dragging his attention back to the golf game, he walked over to where Dave stood watching his wife's swing with a critical eye.

"That's good, honey. You're not pulling your swing as much."

"It felt better," Madison said with a smile.

"The southwest sales aren't where we want them," Josh responded to the earlier question without preamble as Madison returned her club to the bag in the cart, "because we can't guarantee the production side from that area. The sales staff makes the deal, but we keep running into problems with promised deliveries. Our people aren't working together."

Dave snorted. "Is that what your people are claiming? Whining that the production side is to blame?"

"No," Josh said steadily, watching as Madison helped Katie choose a club. "It's my own observation and my own experience. The problem isn't crippling us, but we don't have good flow-through of our orders. It's like the production people have their jobs, their concerns, and we sales people have our concerns. But neither department seems to be getting the big picture."

Dave frowned. "You know I'm responsible for both the sales and production teams in this area?"

"Yes, sir, I do." Josh allowed no hint of apology in his voice. In his opinion, the executive staff neglected getting the viewpoint of the guy in the trenches. The sales-production relationship was too important to ignore any longer, even if some of the executives had to be made uncomfortable.

Beside him, Dave fell silent.

The two men stood to the side of the tee box as Katie set her ball down and prepared to tee off. She held the club Madison had selected for her, placing her hands in an approximation of the grip Josh himself had shown her earlier.

Watching her fixed, cheerful smile, her deep coral golf shirt vivid against the green grass, Josh had to give her points for bravery. The woman wasn't afraid to make a fool of herself, apparently.

She'd never golfed before. Never even set foot on a course. But here she was, responding to his request without complaint, her laughter now just as bright and unselfconscious as if she'd played golf countless times before. She was putting on a good show for him and the others, in spite of the fact that he'd really made her mad.

"Here," Dave said to her, stepping forward. "You need to snug up your grip, some. Now, keep your eye on the ball when you swing."

"Okay." She shifted her feet and squinted toward the green in a playful parody of golfers she must have seen on television. "So now I haul off and whack the ball?"

"Something like that," Josh said dryly, resisting the urge to go over and put his arms around her to "show her" how she should swing. He hadn't even kissed her since they'd made love after the cocktail party, despite an almost constant gnawing urge to touch her again. He'd made his apology this afternoon and knew it had gone over like a lead balloon.

"Just lift the club back," Madison said, her voice gentle. "That's right. Then watch the ball and swing forward."

Katie swung, her club making contact with the ball and lifting it up so that the small white sphere was chucked a pitiful distance down the fairway.

"I hit it!" she said gleefully, swinging around to lift her club over her head with both hands.

Watching her exuberant victory dance in response to what had been a truly terrible drive, Josh smiled, aware of a sudden, urgent need to regain that joyful warmth for himself. He had to get her to forgive him for his foolish misstep. Everyone liked to be appreciated. He knew that, had always kept the maxim in mind in his management style, but with Katie, he kept feeling the urge to slow down his own attraction toward her.

Next to him, Dave chuckled, his natural tendency toward paternal condescension apparently tempered by genuine amusement. "That's the way, Katie. Another three or four of those and you'll be in sight of the green."

Katie stopped dancing long enough to stick her tongue out at him. "I'm within sight of the green now. Another time or two and I'll be good enough at this to go pro."

"That's what I like about you, girl," Dave said with another laugh. "You've got confidence. Can't golf worth a spit, but I like the confidence."

The sound of Katie's responding chuckle sent a trickle of animal attraction down Josh's spine and he walked to the cart, preparing to drive them down to where her ball waited.

It probably wasn't a good idea to get addicted to Katie's brand of sparkling evanescence. Not good to long for her unforgettable lovemaking. There were too many Flanagan drawbacks, even if all they did was have a physical relationship while he went after this promotion. Unquestionably, Katie wasn't Erin. She was much more open than her disloyal sister had ever been, but her other Flanagan characteristics were just as troubling.

Still, he found himself determined to get past the wall she'd put up since their fight. The woman was very angry with him. He knew that, even if she was smiling and laughing with the others, even if she hadn't yelled at him when they'd talked earlier in the car. She'd wanted to, he knew, and at this point, he'd have welcomed a venting of her anger. Anything to clear the air and get her back to being her buoyant self.

Six holes later, Katie sat in the back of the golf cart with Madison while the men walked through the longer grass along the fairway, looking for Dave's ball.

Beside her, Madison sighed.

Glancing at the other woman, Katie detected the hint of a droop to her lovely mouth and noticed again the faint sadness at the back of her eyes.

All morning, Madison had smiled and gamely smacked the golf ball around. All morning Katie had become increasingly aware of the other woman's unhappiness, despite her own discord with Josh.

"Aren't you feeling well today?" Katie asked, unable to ignore her lovely companion's mournful air any longer. "Is something troubling you?"

"Oh!" Madison glanced up, contrition in her eyes. "I'm sorry to be bad company."

"No. You're not bad company; you're sad." Katie leaned forward, placing her hand on the other woman's arm. "What's wrong?"

"Nothing. Really," Madison said, the words apologetic and evasive. "I enjoyed our photo shoot last week."

"I'm glad." Katie smiled encouragingly. "I wanted you to be comfortable."

"Oh, I was." Glancing away, Madison sighed again. "I guess I envy your going after your dreams."

"It's not always easy," Katie replied soberly, thinking of Josh and the tangled mess of emotions between them.

"No, owning your own business takes a lot of work," Madison agreed, looking down at her hands clasped in her lap. "But at least you have a reason to get up every morning."

Startled by the flat note of depression in her companion's words, Katie stared at her, not sure what to say. Between her struggle to get the studio going and her confusion about her feelings with Josh, she didn't really think of her life as being fulfilling and rewarding.

"But . . . you have a wonderful life." The words sounded stupid as soon as they were out of Katie's mouth, but she didn't know how to take them back.

Next to her, Madison moved restlessly before saying ruefully, "I know, I know. You should probably tell me to get over it like Dave does."

An indignant sound escaped Katie's throat before she knew it, drawing Madison's attention.

"He's just trying to help," the other woman defended automatically, her voice tired, "but sometimes I feel like I don't *have* a life. I live Dave's life."

She stopped abruptly, looking over to where her husband swung a club at his golf ball.

Gaping at her in appalled concern, Katie tried to find some adequate phrase to offer. She knew how frustrating it was to feel aimless, not to know where she belonged or what would make her happy. She'd just never thought of someone with Madison's life feeling the same. Yes, the woman had an occasionally irritating husband, but she'd never acted less than satisfied before.

"I shouldn't complain," Madison said, her words quiet. "I have a nice house and car, and a husband who loves and needs me. Some women would kill to have my life."

"But you want more," Katie said slowly.

"Yes."

They fell silent then as the men approached the cart, Dave laughing at some comment of Josh's. With the sun glinting off his dark hair, he looked confident and sexy and altogether infuriating. She wanted to smack him for thinking his boyishly rueful apology made up for the way he'd acted the other morning. The words "I'm sorry" didn't change anything if he still held the same low opinion of her.

But she knew this wasn't the time to let loose on him.

Sitting back as the men drew nearer, Katie's mind flicked through the conversation she'd just had with Madison, impressions and emotions swirling in her head.

"Your turn, honey," Dave called.

His wife was already getting out of the cart.

Katie watched as Josh came to stand next to her side of the golf cart.

"Are you having a good time?" he asked, his gaze steady on her face.

"Yeah, sure," she murmured ironically. "I'm not sure I'll invest a lot of time in chasing a little ball around with a club, but it's okay."

He lowered his voice. "I know and I appreciate your

coming today. Especially since I was such a jerk the other day."

Katie lifted her gaze to his. "You think so?"

"Yes," he said steadily, not responding to the edge in her question.

On the far side of the fairway, Madison took her shot, sending her golf ball sailing toward the circle of brighter green grass.

"Your turn," Josh said, putting out his hand to help her get out of the cart.

Katie placed her hand in his, conscious of the warmth and strength of his grip, conscious of a stupid wave of longing.

But she'd gone over and over it in her head. Maybe caution wasn't her usual watchword, but she refused to be his sexual playtoy. How foolish it would be for her to get further involved with a guy who had a lousy opinion of her. Every time she made love with him, she'd lose a piece of her heart to a man whose life goal focused on never needing anyone. A man who could never again trust his love to a Flanagan.

Crossing the green to where her ball lay, Katie absently nudged the ball toward the cup. After two swipes at it, she managed to scoot the thing into the hole on the third try.

"Well, she's consistent," Dave told Josh in laughing consolation. "Some people just aren't golfers."

"That's not particularly important to me," Josh agreed, his tone dry.

Ignoring them, Katie glanced again to where Madison stood, immaculate in her golf sportswear, a visor with the country club logo perched on her head.

It was so easy to look at someone else's life and assume

it was perfect, that *they* at least had it together. Truthfully, she didn't envy Madison being married to a guy like Dave. He clearly had more than his share of ego and less than one could wish for in the sensitivity category. But people wanted different things out of relationships. Who could blame a young, unsure woman for enjoying the company of an older, more self-confident man?

Climbing back into the golf cart with the others' conversation ebbing around her, Katie pondered the irony of the situation. Madison was right. Many woman would kill to have the comforts she enjoyed.

Only she obviously wasn't enjoying them much.

Josh whipped the cart up a small hill, stopping beside the tee box for the next hole.

Deliberately staying in the cart as Dave and Josh got out, Katie waited till they were several yards away, eyeing up the fairway, before she spoke.

"What do you want to do with your life, Madison?" she asked abruptly. "What's your dream?"

Sitting quietly beside her, the other woman glanced up. She gave a strained laugh. "Don't worry about me. It's not always like this. Usually I'm very content. I'm probably hormonal today or something."

"No!" Katie hissed, casting a cautious glance to where Dave was lining up his shot. "Tell me your dream."

Madison fell silent.

Determined not to let the woman shrug off what Katie was sure was genuine unhappiness, she waited for Madison's response.

Finally, the other woman spoke, the quirk of a self-deprecatory smile on her lips. "I think I want to be a social worker."

"What?" Of all the things she'd imagined, she hadn't come close, Katie thought, startled. The woman was model-beautiful and she wanted to do something as unglamorous as social work?

"I know, I know." Madison lifted a hand to halt the protest she was obviously expecting. "Dave's right. No money. No respect. Dealing with the dregs of humanity. Why would anyone want to be a social worker?"

Dave's voice intruded on their conversation then, heavy with a ponderous playfulness. "Madison! You're next, honey. You girls have got to quit your gabbing and stay with the game."

"Coming," she said, sliding hurriedly out of her seat at the back of the golf cart.

Katie got out more slowly, her mind spinning with possibilities. She hated to see others unhappy or trapped. It never made sense to her not to tackle obstacles. There always had to be a way over or around them.

Why the heck shouldn't Madison be a social worker if she wanted to?

Selecting a club from the bag almost at random, Katie waited until the other woman was done before taking her turn. Dropping the ball onto the tee, she glanced at the green briefly before pulling the club back and swatting at the ball.

"Great shot!" Josh called out a moment later, coming toward her as she casually noted how close her now-rolling ball was to the green.

"Now you're getting it!" Dave bellowed.

Josh stood beside her, his hand near her arm as if to touch her. "That was good. See? Concentration pays off."

Katie didn't immediately respond.

Still standing next to her, his hand now dropped to his side, Josh said shortly, "Are you going to accept my apology or continue sulking? This isn't your best trait, you know. Holding a grudge."

She looked up at him in speechless indignation. *He'd* been a jerk and now she was small-minded for being upset about it?

"I've said I was wrong. Forgive me," he said, more of a demand than a request.

If only he knew what he was apologizing for, Katie thought, getting even more angry.

"Katie?" he said when she didn't respond.

"Sorry," she shot back childishly, "I guess I'm not through sulking!"

"Josh, let's get moving," Dave yelled, for all the world like he was leading a cavalry charge.

Katie turned away, stalking back to the cart with Josh following behind her. They got into the vehicle and moved toward the green.

This time it seemed to Katie as if Madison were waiting for the men to move away from the cart so they could continue their conversation. Tearing her furious thoughts away from the situation with Josh, Katie turned to the other woman.

Without giving her a chance to disclaim her distress again, Katie said abruptly, "Social work is a very worthwhile career. Why can't you be a social worker?"

The other woman's expression was startled. "Well, I'd have to go to college and get a degree."

"So?" Katie demanded, with the confidence in college enrollment she'd garnered from three previous abortive college attempts herself.

Madison shook her head. "It wouldn't work. I know it probably looks like I just spend my life getting my hair and nails done, but we have a lot of social commitments that are important to Dave's career. And I have the house to run and Eden Duchesses's competitions to manage."

"It's just a matter of choices," Katie shot back. "The dog doesn't *have* to compete. It's not like she's going to the Olympics. And you can hire a housekeeper to handle the house. You could still go to school."

A flash of excitement lit Madison's face before fading. She shook her head. "Dave wouldn't like it."

"Why not?" Katie demanded with a hint of belligerence. "If it makes you happy, why would it be a problem for him?"

The other woman paused, flashing her husband a glance. "It would be different if I wanted to do interior design or art. Or even real estate."

"Why?" Katie stared at the woman, uncomprehending.

Madison shrugged as she got out of the golf cart to take her turn. "Business people understand those careers. But social work? Dave would be . . . embarrassed."

"That's ridiculous!" Katie said, following her. "There's nothing wrong with being a social worker. I was raised by a single mother who sometimes had trouble making ends meet. When I was a kid, we had to make use of social programs a time or two. I have nothing but good things to say about social workers."

Madison looked up at her with an arrested expression.

Feeling as though the words were propelled out of her, Katie continued, "You can't let Dave tell you what to do to make your life fulfilling. If you don't follow your own dream, you have no one to blame but yourself."

"I-I'm not blaming him," Madison stammered.

"Then why aren't you going to school to be a social worker?" Katie retorted, remembering at the last minute to lower her voice.

"I guess"—Madison drew a deep breath—"I guess I am."

After the other woman sunk her ball into the hole, Katie took the putter Dave handed her and went to where her own ball lay. Giving it a hearty *thwack,* she overshot the hole.

"Gently," Josh called out, a mocking note in his voice.

Eyeing the small, round hole, she gritted her teeth, concentrated on batting the ball in—and missed again.

"Damnation," she muttered, finally scooting the ball in.

"Darling!" Josh said, walking up to her with that taunting glint in his eyes. "Congratulations!"

Without warning, he seized her in his arms, lowering his mouth onto hers. In the space of seconds, she found herself being ruthlessly kissed, the heat of his muscled body against hers, the skill of his mouth demanding on hers. Conscious of Dave and Madison not ten feet away, Katie knew if she fought Josh's kiss, their whole charade would go up in smoke. He knew it, too! The bastard.

Holding still and stiff beneath the onslaught of his kiss, she felt the blood roaring in her ears with a sudden, betraying quickening of her body to his. Then, when she thought she might be able to hold out against the lure of his touch, his kiss became gentle. Stroking her mouth with the soft wooing of his lips, he courted her sweetly, melting her resistance. She felt herself softening in his arms, her body curving into his.

"Come on, you two lovebirds!" Dave said raucously. "We've got three more holes to play."

Nine

Josh pulled his car to a stop in front of Katie's apartment, acutely aware of how furious she was after he'd kissed her on the golf course.

She sat in the seat next to him, stiff and silent, her slender, golden legs crossed, her face stony. All day he'd been aware of her, taunted by her nearness and her infuriating refusal to forgive him.

She was madder than a wet hen, but he couldn't regret that kiss. He'd wanted to touch Katie all day and hadn't until the very end. With an iron will, he'd kept his hands to himself, his thoughts chasing themselves around in his head like racers at the Indy.

What had he done that was so bad? Made fun of her "cooking"? Not gone down on one knee when she'd saved his damned cocktail party? Okay! She'd done a great job with the gathering and he'd told her he appreciated it. Still, she'd stormed out of his apartment the morning after they made love as if he'd committed one of the seven deadly sins. What was that all about?

He had to admit he didn't understand her. The weird part was how much, at this instant, he wanted to. He could no longer tell himself she was his ex-fiancée's lightweight sister and nothing more. She seemed like *more*.

Despite himself, he was curious about her in ways he didn't quite understand.

She opened the car door suddenly, gathering her purse and sweater without a word.

Josh acted on a swift impulse, reaching his hand out to catch her by the arm. "Have dinner with me tonight."

"Dinner?" She flashed him a hostile glance. "You have a business function tonight?"

"No," he admitted, aware that he was feeling his way into uncharted territory. "Just . . . have dinner with me."

For once, she seemed caught completely off-guard.

"Why? So you can manhandle me in public again?" she snarled.

"No," he said, determined not to apologize for the kiss. "Because I want to spend time with you."

She looked at him, surprise springing into her blue eyes at his simple admission. Katie's hesitating gaze searched his face as if trying to read his sincerity.

"Please," he offered softly.

Her gaze fell away from his as she glanced down at her golf outfit. "I need to shower and change."

Josh tried to ignore the relief that surged through him at her inferred acceptance. "So do I. How about I pick you up in an hour?"

"An hour and a half," she amended with a hint of her saucy grin before opening the car door and walking toward her apartment door.

He watched her go, hardly aware of the foolish smile on his face, lifting his hand in response to her little wave before she disappeared inside.

Putting the car into reverse, he left the parking lot, not

realizing until he was halfway down the street that he was whistling.

She hadn't seen Josh in such low-class surroundings since the old days, and even then not often, since Erin had always sought the most expensive entertainment available to her.

Katie propped her chin on her hand, her elbow on the table between them and squinted at him through the dim light of the cheesy candle stuck in a wine bottle. She loved this pizza joint. Despite its budget prices, the food here made it one of the area's best kept secrets.

Josh's kiss on the golf course had shaken her down to her toes. How she could melt in his arms when she was so angry with him, she couldn't fathom. But afterward, in the car, he'd seemed to really want her to spend the evening with him and his sincerity disarmed her anger. As a reward for the efforts he was making to atone for his stupidity after the cocktail party, she'd decided to introduce him to Lino's Pizza and Pasta.

What a mistake her sister had made when she'd bailed out on Josh Morgan, Katie mused, looking at him across the table. With his determination to reach the top, he seemed perfect for Erin—except for how *wrong* her sister was for him.

Thank heavens Erin had come to the same conclusion. She seemed completely uninterested in Josh's romantic pursuits—even if they concerned her own sister. That was not a surprise, really, since she'd never loved the man.

"You've been here before," Josh said, watching the

waitress retreat with their order. "How long till the pizza arrives?"

"Fifteen minutes. They do a quick turnaround because most of their clientele wants takeout. Gotta be fast." She smiled at him, furiously hoping he couldn't see the crazy jitteriness that kept her wanting to chew on her lip.

There was nothing to be nervous about. They'd made love together and she wasn't sure it had even meant anything to him. End of story. Their deal hadn't included falling in love. Now that he'd apologized for dissing her party efforts, they could get back on a businesslike footing. Still, she couldn't keep her heart from beating faster with him this near, couldn't help but think of how good *they* would be together. More than the sex, as incredible as that had been. More than the pretending.

Josh leaned back against the booth seat, looking younger and more relaxed than she ever remembered. He wore another golf shirt, open at the neck, the navy-blue knit echoing the dark color of his eyes. But unlike this morning, his smile seemed easier.

For her, the worst part of going to his business functions was that when he was there, Josh didn't seem like himself. He was not the confident, relaxed man she saw across the table from her. In his work setting, Josh was still as confident, but she saw a tension in him, a stress that worried her.

"So how's business at the studio?"

His question startled her, uttered as it was in a friendly tone completely unlike his previous scathing references to the place she loved.

"Good. Very good. I've had a full schedule since Madison got me the club directory job."

He nodded, the candlelight glowing on his face. "It must be very satisfying. Particularly since you had such strong feelings about continuing with your grandfather's work."

"Yes," she said simply. "I feel his presence in the place and I imagine him watching me and smiling."

Across the table, Josh seemed to study her. "I never knew him, you know. He must have been quite a man to have inspired this affection."

"He was the best," Katie agreed, her vision misting slightly. Grandfather would have liked Josh.

"Tell me about him," Josh invited.

"Well, no matter what happened, he was always there for us. Things were rocky sometimes. My mother didn't make much money and sometimes the things she tried her hand at didn't do well, but we were happy. Loved. Grandfather was a big part of that."

"But you moved around a lot," he pointed out. "That's very unsettling to children."

"Not all children," she disagreed. "I liked going into new schools, meeting the kids. Figuring out which teachers could be played and which you had to really work for."

She sent him a sly smile. "I got pretty good at that sort of thing."

"I'm sure you did." His words were dry. "But what kind of education did you get? Not all school districts are teaching the same thing at the same time. There had to have been some gaps to be made up."

"I managed," she said blithely. "Teachers usually liked me, except the ones who got their knickers in a twist if you talked in class. The thing that got me in trouble the most, though, was asking questions."

He frowned. "Aren't you supposed to ask questions in school?"

"Some questions, yes," Katie agreed. "But I used to ask the insubordinate ones sometimes, like, 'If this is an opinion question, why is your opinion more right than mine?' "

"Oh." Josh laughed. "One of those students, were you?"

"Yes," she confirmed, her tone as demure as she could manage. "And when I got into trouble, I learned to call my grandfather to deal with the principal. My mother tended to be even more radical than I was."

"Your grandfather really was your father figure, wasn't he?"

"Yes." Katie pleated the paper napkin on the table in front of her.

"Your own father hasn't been around much in your life?" Josh's gently searching glance held a hint of awkwardness, as if he were checking to make sure she didn't find the question too painful.

Katie smiled at the thought. Josh in a sensitive moment? It had to be her imagination. He wouldn't know his own feelings if they bit him and even then, she suspected he'd think they didn't matter. But then maybe it was only he who couldn't stray into emotionally murky territory? Maybe since she was a woman and a Flanagan, she was allowed.

"No, my father isn't in my life." She shrugged, the old wounds now only slightly painful. "But I've still had it better than some kids. My mother doesn't have the most common sense, but she's loving. Heck, some kids don't have *one* parent. . . ."

He looked down as her voice trailed off, his face somber.

"Oh, Josh," she said breathlessly, "that was so thoughtless of me. I'm sorry."

"It's all right," he responded, glancing up with a rueful smile tugging at his lips, an echoing gleam in his eyes. "You get to a certain point and your childhood seems far away. My lot could have been worse."

"Not much," she objected, her voice tart. "From the things I've heard—"

"It wasn't that hard," he cut in dismissively.

"—you didn't have it much better than Cinderella. And it must have been harder on you than your brother since you were the older one."

His smile seemed almost tender as his gaze lingered on her face. "Thanks for the support, but I learned from adversity. Of course, I also built things up in my head from time to time. About how much different it would be, how much better everything would be if my parents had been alive."

"That's natural," she said softly.

"Oh, yes." His tone was light now. "I'm sure my dreams helped me get through that difficult time, but as an adult, you have to remember not to confuse fantasy and reality. Life involves a certain amount of hardship, even when you have parents. I'm sure my early trials have helped me come as far as I have in the world."

Your childhood's not as far away as you think, she wanted to say, remembering the tension in his jaw when he played golf with Dave and when he escorted her to those damn business dinners.

Intuition told her their charade didn't sit well with him.

Josh had always been a straight arrow. Honor and integrity meant a lot to him. Why else would he have offered to marry a pregnant, abandoned woman? Katie knew it had to go against his grain to pretend to be something he wasn't in this situation. And yet, he was doing it. Deliberately pretending to be something other than what he was. Breaching his own integrity.

That spoke more than anything of his unresolved issues, in Katie's mind. She shouldn't care, shouldn't let herself give in to the love and longing he raised in her. But it seemed unavoidable.

"I-I can't imagine how horrible that time must have been for you," she said, "how devastating. But do you really think success and money will make up for all of the past?"

Josh's laugh sounded easy. "No, of course not. But then, it's not supposed to. The past is past."

"Really?" She knew her skepticism shimmered on her face.

"Yes, really." The amused tolerance on his face seemed genuine. "Who wouldn't want success and money? The whole world is chasing after it. Even you."

She looked at him for a long moment, wondering if he really didn't know what motivated him to betray his own nature. "Yes, I want some success. Enough money to keep the studio going, to bring it back to life. Enough to keep me supplied with cat food for my beasts and to pay the rent."

Josh's smile widened as though she'd confirmed his observation.

"But you want more," she said gently. "A lot more."

"Bigger beasts," he agreed, laughing again. "Higher rent. It pretty much comes to the same thing."

Josh shifted in his chair, trying to keep his boredom from seeping onto his face. Watkins had covered this point adequately twenty minutes ago, but still the fool droned on. Would this meeting never end?

Noon had come and gone a half-hour ago and, in the face of his complete disinterest in Watkins's assessments, lunch sounded particularly appetizing.

This was the worst of corporate America. Meetings with no real point, and more meetings to discuss the previous meetings.

Holding his pad at a better angle, Josh added mouse ears to the creature he'd been doodling and tried to decide which project he'd work on first when he was finally released from this purgatory.

". . . in the steepest part of our acquisition curve and, as I said, we appear to be keeping up . . . ," Watkins was droning.

Absorbed in giving the mouse creature an interestingly female shape, Josh didn't immediately hear the quiet tapping at the conference room door. He did notice, however, when Rick left the table to see what was wanted.

True to form, Watkins never hesitated in his presentation and the poor suckers near the head of the table appeared to be making a valiant attempt to care.

At the door, Rick's body shielded whomever was seeking entrance.

Josh had an uncharacteristic urge to shout out to the

intruder to *run!* rather than risk being drawn into the vortex of Watkins's lethal report.

Glancing down to add a lush curve of hip to his voluptuous rodent, he didn't know he was being summoned to the door until Felicia, who was sitting next to him at the table, nudged him with her elbow. He dropped his pad on the table, automatically covering it with the meeting agenda he'd been given.

Careful to roll his chair back as quietly as possible, he went frowning to the door where Rick stood, a goofy smile on his face.

Through the gap left by the partially opened door, Josh could see his secretary, Sara Harper, smiling at him, too.

He moved through the door, leaving the conference room to keep from disturbing the meeting. Even if Watkins was reciting the alphabet, no intelligent person disturbed the natural progression of a meeting. The more disruption, the longer the darn thing went on, and he didn't want to earn his coworkers' wrath.

Out in the hallway, the door carefully closed behind him, he saw Katie standing next to Sara.

"Katie!" He turned to her with a flash of anxiety. "What are you doing here? Is something wrong?"

"I'm sorry if this interruption is untimely," Sara said with a twinkle in her eye, "but I remembered Watkins was leading out and I thought you might not mind talking to your fiancée."

"It's fine," he reassured his secretary, his hand seeming to automatically find Katie's arm.

"Good. Well, I'll get back to my desk."

"When are you having lunch?" he called after her, remembering the older woman's borderline hypoglycemia as she retreated.

"I went an hour ago," she responded with another smile before disappearing around a corner.

His attention reverting to Katie, he realized he still held her, his hand clasping her arm just above her elbow. The sensation of her smooth, firm skin filtered into his mind at that instant.

Their dinner the other night had been an indication of a healing of the breach between them, but afterward she hadn't invited him into her apartment to enjoy the heaven of her body. He'd regained her warm smiles, but still didn't have the right to touch her.

Behaving with discipline, he released her immediately, letting his hand fall to his side.

"Hi," he said, asking again, "is anything wrong?"

The last time she'd come to his office—weeks ago, with the intention of wheedling him into agreeing to her plans for the studio—she'd dressed much more formally. He'd liked that cream-colored suit a lot, but today's outfit had the bonus of showing much more skin.

"Everything's fine," she assured him, her sunny smile brightening the corridor. She was wearing a snug pair of jeans and a white-flowered top that ended an inch above the jeans.

Josh tried not to think about that bare inch of midriff.

"Why are you here?" he blurted out, unable to think of anything smoother to say since most of his brain seemed to be thinking about her bare midriff and all the other bare possibilities.

The casual tumble of her red hair piled on the top of

her head in a charmingly haphazard fashion, Katie smiled at him.

"Actually," she said, drawing closer to him and speaking in a lowered voice, "there is something wrong."

"What?" he asked, his alarm subsiding. If the studio had burned down, Katie wouldn't look so relaxed.

She leaned forward, brushing against him to whisper in his ear, "You've been working too hard."

"What?" he asked again, this time his mind fogged by the reaction brought on by her fresh scent and the sensation of her clothed breast grazing his arm.

"Working too hard," she said slowly, as if he were developmentally delayed. But the charming smile on her face and the teasing light in her blue eyes gave him his first real clue.

She was here to waste his time, as surely as Watkins was wasting his time—only Katie promised to do so in much more enjoyable ways. No matter what the subject, Katie would *always* be more entertaining than Watkins.

"You're working late every night," she told him, a playful hint of sternness in her face. "I bet that golf game a week ago was the last daylight you've seen."

"Don't be ridiculous," Josh said even as he recognized the truth of her accusation. *She knew when he worked late?*

Very conscious of her closeness, the nearness of her body, he savored the sensations she sent through him. He felt a jolt of heat and hunger that had nothing to do with his skipping lunch.

"You're becoming a workaholic," she said, lowering her voice on the last word as she glanced up and down the hall as if she was concerned about being overheard.

"Listen, the goal is in sight," he told her, his excitement at the thought barely suppressed as he drew her further away from the conference room door. "Dave hinted at it on Monday. I'm being seriously considered for this promotion."

Katie's face lit up. "That's great. Wonderful! I have not played golf in vain!"

He couldn't help chuckling at her silliness. "No. It was a worthwhile sacrifice."

"That's terrific news," she said, stepping to the side as a woman passed them in the corridor. "And it's all the more reason for you to come with me quietly now."

"Come with you?"

Katie glanced at the woman's retreating back. "I'm here to kidnap you."

He looked down at her, not sure he'd heard her soft words correctly. "Huh?"

She grinned. "I have it all arranged. I'm kidnapping you for a picnic this afternoon."

"Don't be ridiculous," he said, the words testy. "I've got work to do this afternoon."

"That's my point," she said with a hint of triumph. "You've *always* got work to do. I'm beginning to think you could work twenty-four-seven and still find work to do."

Her exaggeration and the playfulness he saw on her expressive face brought an answering gleam to his face. He felt his lips trying to twitch into a grin and quickly subdued the insurrection.

"That's all the more reason not to succumb to the urge to randomly picnic," he deadpanned.

"But you never succumb to those urges," she hissed,

leaning close enough that he could drag in the breath she'd just released.

Josh looked down at her, sensation bolting through him as he thought of all the other urges he'd been resisting in the past two weeks. Like the urge to storm into the studio and take her on that damn satin-covered bed. The urge to call her late at night just to hear her voice.

She was getting to him, damn it, and he couldn't let that happen. Katie was the most Flanagan of all the Flanagans and he'd been bitten big-time before; but he still found himself daydreaming about the sound of her laughter.

"So that's why I'm here," she said, as if the conclusion was obvious. Her hand still on his arm, she tugged him further away from the door. "Let's get going."

"Now?" He should resist—Josh knew that.

"Yes. Now."

He held firm against her urging hands, an act that cost him a lot of self-control. "I can't leave the meeting."

"Why not? Are you leading it?" she asked innocently.

"No." He couldn't let her get to him. But a rebellious part of him wanted to cast his concentrated effort aside for a while and lie in the sun with her. Surely, that wouldn't be so bad.

"If you're not leading the meeting, you're leaving," she said, still pulling him toward the main hallway.

"Katie," he said, exasperation mingling with an amusement he couldn't deny. "Wait."

"No." She drew him around the corner and turned him toward the elevators. With a slender arm around his waist, she urged him along like a kindergarten teacher with a small, reluctant boy.

Only he wasn't small, and he couldn't come close to summoning up reluctance.

"It's lunchtime," she said firmly. "The world won't fall apart if you have lunch in the park."

"God, this is wonderful," he murmured.

Beside her, Josh lay back on the quilt, with the strong spring sunshine dappling through the trees and the green grass like a sea all around them.

This small area of the Botanical Gardens was dedicated to the butterflies, Katie knew. Here and there lantana grew, and in the small corner of the garden, walled on three sides, was a pond surrounded with rocks. Clumps of perennials bloomed in the sunlight.

On this quiet Wednesday, the place was empty save the two of them and the small yellow creature poised on Josh's knee, its wings opening and closing. Around them lay discarded remains of their takeout "picnic," the cartons and napkins spilling off the quilt.

The air was still and quiet, poured over with the bright pure sunlight of spring that was still untouched by summer's scalding heat. It was almost as if she could breathe the sunlight into her lungs, as if she had, and it had left her dizzy and giddy.

"Look how bright it is," he murmured as if trying not to disturb the butterfly that opened and closed its small yellow wings on his knee, practicing some strange form of butterfly calisthenics. "Sunlight. I'd forgotten about the sun."

"I know," Katie said in mock sadness, careful to keep the surge of love out of her voice. She loved him, and her heart contracted within her. He might be an uptight business geek, but he had a steadfast quality, a strength that drew her. When he gave his heart to a woman, there'd be no going back.

"That's why I insisted on you coming," she teased. "We can't have you turning into a pale, sunless thing."

"It's a problem lots of executives have," he agreed, watching as his insect companion rose and fluttered above his knee. "They have to install tanning booths in some buildings just to keep us from looking like vampires. Sometimes they schedule meetings at different buildings just so we have to walk to our cars in the sun and catch some exposure."

Katie smiled at his uncharacteristic silliness, knowing it was foolishness to love him. He'd made his negative views about her more than clear. Never again would he formally involve himself with a member of her family. Sure, he now claimed her as a fiancée, but they both knew the falsity of it, just as she knew she represented to him the polar opposite of the stability he craved.

But loving him was as unavoidable as it was foolish.

She watched him steadily now, the shifting shadows from the trees overhead blurring into a kind of dusky umbrella around them. Despite his lighthearted banter, she saw the fatigue on his face, the shadows still in his eyes. How did a man get to be so driven by his demons?

As if her love tied her to him with some powerful connection, she'd known he was working himself harder than ever. She'd called his apartment several evenings this past week with nothing specific to say to him, and had been unsurprised that his phone rang repeatedly until the machine picked up. She'd have bet he hadn't fallen into bed until ten o'clock or later each night.

This was how a man prepared himself for a heart attack at age forty-five.

Lying beside her now, his dark head propped on his arms crossed behind him, he seemed as if he'd given himself permission to relax. Just these few, small hours.

He needed this and she needed to give it to him, needed to be a small influence for good in his life somehow. This job of his would kill him eventually, would grow even more lethal the higher he climbed—lethal to his spirit, even if his body managed to survive until retirement.

The butterfly returned, flitting up to land delicately on Josh's stomach this time.

"Well, hello." He watched the creature with a small boy's quiet intensity.

"Josh? If you didn't do this kind of work, what else would you like to do?"

He glanced away from the butterfly, frowning. "If I didn't have this job? Get another one, I guess."

"But what other careers?" she asked, stretching out beside him on the quilt, lying on her side to look at his face.

Shrugging, he said, "I've worked in the telecommunications industry since I got my degree in business. If I didn't work for this company, I'd get a job with another one."

"But if you could do *anything?* Come on, play the game with me. Would you be a rock star, a ball coach, a train driver—"

Josh laughed. "You mean an engineer? The guy that drives the train's engine?"

"That," she said, impatient with his nit-picking, "or an astronaut, maybe? Heck, maybe you really want to be a shoe salesman!"

"No," he said with complete certainty.

"Some men think women's feet are sexy," she teased, lifting her bare foot to stroke over his trousered calf. "Feet aren't your thing?"

The intensity in his face as he looked down to where her foot brushed along his leg, left her feeling suddenly winded. She felt the stillness between them, the sunlight seeming to have become boiling hot around them.

"Well then," she said, her voice still breathless, "maybe you'd like to be a race car driver. You'd get to drive a hundred miles per hour and never get a ticket."

"Are these your fantasies?" he asked suddenly, his voice dry as his gaze swung up to her face. "If so, you have the dreams of a twelve-year-old boy."

"Well, what are yours?" she insisted. "What did you want to be when you were twelve?"

"I don't remember," he said slowly, turning his head so that he stared into the ambient space above him. "Nothing too specific. I wanted money. A nice house. A family of my own to come home to every night. You know, like the old reruns of television sitcoms."

Rolling onto her back, Katie scooted her head over near his, as if to see what he saw above him. "So, when you came home at night, what were you wearing?"

He turned his head, sending her a rueful, teasing glance. *"Very* like a twelve-year-old boy."

"I'm serious," she said with an answering smile. Did you come home every day at the same time? Were you wearing a suit and tie or bathing trunks or—"

"An astronaut's uniform," he finished. "I understand."

Katie scooted her head closer to his, so that they lay on the quilt like two petals of the same flower. "Tell me."

"I guess," he said slowly, "I've always been wearing a suit and tie."

"Did you carry a briefcase? Like in *Father Knows Best?*"

"Yes."

"And you came home at the same time every night?"

"Yes." His responses became more clipped with each question.

"Did you get to decide when you came home?" she asked.

"I guess," he said slowly.

A quick glance out of the corner of her eye told Katie he was frowning, as if the game they played displeased him.

"So you were in business, but you were your own boss?"

His laugh was short and not particularly amused. "Isn't that what most people want?"

"No," she asserted firmly, "that's too much responsibility for most people. They want money, freedom of schedule and nothing to worry about when they come home."

Lying next to her, he said nothing.

"But you love responsibility," she continued, saying the words softly.

"I'm comfortable with it," he agreed, his tone neutral.

"Maybe too comfortable."

Josh straightened, propping himself on one elbow as he studied her face. "What do you mean?"

"You're always working, never just being. With the exception of this afternoon, I've never seen you *not* working during the day. Even when you were golfing, you were working."

He made no immediate response, but she could feel his gaze still on her face.

"Maybe," she suggested, throwing caution to the wind, "maybe all this work keeps you from thinking too much, keeps you from remembering things you—"

"Have I ever told you how incredibly beautiful you are?" he said, interrupting ruthlessly.

Katie's gaze swung to his and clung, her breath suddenly feeling tight in her chest. "No."

"Well, you are," he declared, the thread of dispassion in his voice contradicted by the glowing heat she saw in his eyes. "More beautiful than I remember—every time I see you. It's like I've forgotten from the last time. Like I'm surprised every time."

Staring up at him, her gaze locked with his, she felt mesmerized, stunned by what she heard in his voice, read on his face.

Josh lifted his hand, stroking a finger over her eyebrow. "Delicate. Golden like the sun has kissed you all over."

Longing and need swept over her, forest fire-style. She knew his kisses, remembered the exact feel of his mouth on her . . . and it had been so long. Days.

The very oxygen in the small garden seemed to have solidified around them, caught in a golden bubble, slow to seep into her lungs. Time spaced out to an impossibly delayed ticking of seconds.

Josh lowered his mouth to hers, his lips warm from the sun, tasting of sorrows and promises broken, begging for a love she knew his mind couldn't accept.

Ten

Lifting her hand, she held him to her, his mouth against hers, the short feathery smoothness of his hair against her palm.

She loved him. And loving him, she needed to give him everything—to try and thaw out his cold, lonely heart. She knew the risks all too well. But some risks had to be taken, no matter what the cost.

God, he felt good; his kiss tasted of surrender and connection, of some desperate need to still the words between them. Lazily their tongues met, their breath joining. She felt herself curve toward him on the quilt, her body drawn to his like a flower's face to the sun. Pulling her to him, he slid his arm behind her back and braced her for the rhythm of his tongue against hers, the breathless, drugging wonder of his mouth mating with hers.

One hot kiss followed another, slow and thorough, consumed in a magic she couldn't deny. Maybe he would deny it, later. But she knew as she lay beside him, her leg slipped between his, his broad shoulders sheltering them both, that she had to do this. Had to be with him, to try and reach his soul somehow, before he traded it away.

The singing birds, the faint rustling of the leaves overhead, everything faded and she was locked in his embrace, one kiss following another.

He slid a hand under her shirt, kneading one aching breast until she sobbed in pleasure, the sound desperate in her throat.

Josh lifted his head then, taking his mouth from hers to look down at her with passion-dark eyes. For a long moment their gazes met, scorching hot with question and answer.

Do you really want this? he seemed to be asking.

Yes. Yes, I do, she telegraphed back, sure only of this.

Slowly he withdrew his hand from under her shirt, his finger moving over the crest of her nipple. Bending, he pressed one last brief kiss against her mouth and got up from the quilt.

In total silence, they gathered up their trash and folded the blanket. He draped the bulky bundle over one arm, catching her hand in his as they walked to his car.

No words, she thought, almost desperately as they crossed the vivid emerald grass. No words to break this spell, nothing to drive away the magic. Not yet.

He drove to her apartment and followed her up the sidewalk. The clank of her keys against the door as she unlocked it sounded loud in her ears. Pushing the door open, she turned and looked at him as he followed her inside. She absolutely wouldn't apologize for the scatter of magazines on the floor next to the chair. Wouldn't let herself see his sure disapproval of her funky collection of yard-sale furniture, each piece a treasure in her eyes. It wasn't as if he'd never been to her place before.

Nothing in her place matched. Nothing, that is, except them. While as opposite as the poles, still she knew that they balanced each other, even though she'd given up on his ever seeing it.

He stood next to her as she closed the door, his gaze clinging to her in a way that told her he didn't give a damn about the room.

"This way," she said, her voice rusty as though the silence between them left her unsure how to speak. Taking his hand in hers, she led him to her bedroom.

Here, he did glance around, pausing just inside her room. Her old-fashioned vanity sat in one corner, littered with makeup and combs. Several pairs of shoes had collected in the one chair, but none of the disarray mattered now. Katie knew that from the way his gaze bounced back to her face, everything else was disregarded.

Releasing him, she walked into the room and turned to face him. Her gaze locked with his, she lifted the hem of her shirt and drew it over her head. Now without looking at him, she reached behind to unfasten the clasp of her bra. She remembered so well how he'd wrestled with it last time.

To her accustomed fingers, the hooks came free and she took the straps down her arms, looking again into his face. He was still standing by the door, with his face tightened now, his stare seeming to heat her body with the force of his longing.

She reached for the snap on her jeans, aware that he'd moved closer and had reached out a hand to cup her breast. The heat in his fingers sent a shiver through her. Unzipping her jeans, she pushed them down, underwear and all, until she stood before him, naked as she could be. Her sandals came off when she kicked her pants away, and not an inch of her was hidden from his view.

He bent and pressed his mouth against her shoulder, his hands supporting her breasts. Letting her head loll back, Katie lost herself to his touch, to the slow stroking of his thumbs over her nipples, the damp, hot sweep of his mouth.

Then she had to have him bare with her, had to feel his heated skin under hers rather than the irritating primness of his starched shirt. He'd left his jacket in the car, having discarded it before their picnic. Now she opened his shirt, heedless of buttons, impatient with the belt buckle that guarded his waist.

Eventually, she had him stripped. They stood near the foot of her bed, kissing and touching. Slowly their mouths came together, only to part and venture off on exquisitely sensitive trails. He suckled at her breast, his fingers toying between her legs, while she skated her fingers along his length. Then, cupping his tight fanny in both her hands, she pressed herself against him, breasts to his hard chest, belly to his arousal, her open mouth pressed to his.

He lifted her, placing her on the bed and climbing onto it himself to kneel between her knees. There may have been times for flirting and teasing, times to make love against the wall or explore all the other possible connections. But this moment was about merging, about absorbing him into herself until he felt as much a part of her as she did of him.

She wanted full contact, wanted to be able to hold him in her arms, to be sheltered beneath his body as they joined. Scooting back on her bed, she spread her legs and urged him forward, drew him to where his erection met the emptiness in her.

When he thrust home, she felt the ripple of their contact

as if skin melded to skin. No matter that the condom shielded them both. No matter.

He thrust in and sent her hurtling into another place. Pleasure and completion. A connection of bodies beyond the gasping, sobbing urgency. Over and over, he drove into her as she clung to him, meeting his thrusts, begging him for more.

So right, so perfect. Nothing on earth had ever felt so good.

The building, pounding rhythm left them both struggling to draw in breath fast enough. She heard the harshness of his panting breath mingling with hers, the only sound in the room rising above the protests of her mattress. Straining together, lost to everything but the glory between them, Katie felt herself rising to the peak and hurtled over it with Josh in her arms.

Never had a moment been so much about love. Her love, if not his.

The next morning, Josh typed in the last line of the sales report and clicked the button to E-mail it to his group.

The Styrofoam cup of coffee sitting next to his mouse pad reflected an unattractive oily sheen under the fluorescent lights. The coffee in it had gone cold an hour ago and it was now only seven-thirty in the morning.

He sat back in his chair rubbing a hand over his face.

Two hours of solid work and he'd almost made up for his stolen afternoon of passion.

His mouth firmed into a grim line. Might as well call it an afternoon of insanity. He still couldn't believe he'd walked out on a meeting and then allowed himself to spend the next three hours in Katie's warm bed. The time he should have been working, instead spent loving them both into a state of mindless bliss.

He'd come back to the office later, of course. On his desk, he'd found his "notes" from the meeting. Compliments of Rick, no doubt. But three misspent hours left him with an urgency to catch up.

Early this morning, he'd come into the empty office with only the computers' hum and the occasional hush of the building's climate control to disturb the silence.

Yesterday's damn meeting might have been a waste of his time, but he still couldn't believe he'd chucked it. After so many years of following the same rigid work ethic, finding himself shrugging off responsibility didn't sit well with him.

Still, he smiled to himself. It had been beautiful, his passionate picnic with Katie. Like moments stolen out of time. Yes, he'd had to come in this morning at an early hour, but damn. Katie in his arms. Her soft laughter, the glow in her eyes when she looked at him.

For some reason, when he was with her like that, he felt powerful and intelligent. Definitely not above being teased, but always more of a man than he suspected any male could be.

She made him feel like that. For all her flighty, unreliable tendencies and her checkered past, she could bring the most golden moments to life. Her teasing, unpredictable silliness left a trail of warmth through his days, his weeks. There was a single, quicksilver thread of Katie moments that left him hungry for more, even when she was angry with him.

Sitting back in his chair, the quirk of a smile tugging at

his lips, he laughed softly, thinking of her inane teasing yesterday when they'd both returned to earth after the passion. She was an amazing woman; so sexy, so much fun, so wonderful to share with. . . .

Josh brought his careening thoughts to a thudding halt, swallowing hard. Hell, what was he thinking? Here he sat mooning over this woman, aching to hear the reassurance of her voice. Thinking of her as if they had a future together.

Grabbing the cold cup of coffee, he took a bitter gulp and nearly gagged. Josh replaced the cup and rubbed his eyes and tried to focus on the computer screen, tried to gather his scattered wits and do something useful.

He wasn't actually thinking of *being* with her, was he? Where the hell was this all leading? This mushy, moon-struck, stupidity that took hold of him when he thought of her?

She was Katie Flanagan. Sister of Erin Flanagan, who'd dumped him for his own brother after he'd offered to marry her for her child's sake. And then she'd stiffed him for the money he'd loaned to resurrect her family business. For all her undeniable attractions, Katie had an even worse track record of bailing out on men. These were Flanagans here. Genetically incapable of rational, decent lives.

And Katie was the flightiest, the least reliable of them all. How long before she tired of playing at photography and moved to Colorado to teach skiing? Was he asking to be left at the altar like the other men she'd dumped?

Drawing in a sharp breath, Josh realized the thought of being dumped by Katie brought an entirely new kind of emotion to him. Was it all-consuming fury? Agony? When Erin had thrown his chivalry back in his face, running off with his brother the way she had, he'd felt like a fool. But, Katie, she was . . . so much more.

Jerking his thoughts away from the troubling realization, he sorted through the pile of papers on his desk. This was stupid. He'd come in to get some work done. Forcing himself to focus, he began organizing the data in front of him and formulating a timeline for accomplishing the group's goals.

Half an hour later, a hard knock at his open door brought his head up. There in the doorway stood Dave Williams, his lips formed into a tight, unpleasant smile.

"Good morning," Josh said calmly, aware of the signs of trouble on the other man's face.

"So you're here this morning?" The question was coated in sarcasm.

Like everything else, Josh thought tiredly, the man overplayed his delivery. But by disappearing in the middle of a workday without notifying anyone, Josh had earned a certain amount of his boss's displeasure.

"Yes, I'm here," he responded, refusing to tell the jerk that he'd stayed in the office until eight o'clock last night and had been here since five-thirty this morning. Offering excuses wouldn't help. He could take his medicine without whining.

"I thought," Dave said nastily, "maybe after sliding out on the planning meeting, you'd find other ways to amuse yourself this morning. Like picking out china patterns with your fiancée."

China patterns? What the hell was that about?

"No, sir," Josh replied, tacking on the respectful tag as a means of covering his growing irritation. "That sales report you wanted is in your in box."

Giving him a long, hard stare, Dave stepped further into his office, shutting the door behind him. "You know, Morgan, you can't be too careful. I don't have to tell you the decision on that promotion is coming up soon. You've got to get your priorities straight."

"I believe they are straight," Josh said, his voice stiff. For one damn afternoon, he was going to lose the promotion? He didn't think so.

"Well," Dave said, sitting in the chair opposite Josh's desk, "I always thought you had them straight. But this promotion is a big jump for you. A whole new level."

"Yes," Josh said evenly. He was damned if he would grovel for this ass. The thought made his stomach turn. Hadn't they missed a similar damn meeting to play golf the week before?

"A whole new level," the older man repeated. "You know business is not unlike politics. To succeed, a man has to have a settled life with a wife who understands what the job requires."

"Yes?" Josh felt a prickling along his neck. This was the man's second reference to Katie.

"You know," Dave said, adjusting his one knee widely over the other, "Katie's a sexy young thing and I can certainly understand why you're interested in her."

His hearty laugh held a lewd note and Josh was surprised he didn't wink.

"Hell," Dave went on, "who wouldn't be interested in a piece—woman—that well shaped?"

Josh wrestled suddenly with an almost overwhelming urge to smash his fist into his boss's face before flinging him bodily out of his office. Unable to speak calmly, he said nothing, waiting to see what the man's point was. Experience told him that he'd get there eventually.

"Yes," Dave said, "I understand your interest, but she doesn't seem to get it, doesn't have a grip on what we require of our women."

Waiting still, one brow lifted, Josh puzzled over the direction of the man's conversation. Was he suggesting it was Katie's fault he'd cut out on the meeting? And that was why she was suddenly a good lay, but not good wife material?

"That dress she wore to the awards dinner? Those sequins?" Dave shook his head. "It's hard for some people to . . . to understand how to climb the ladder."

Josh clenched his teeth against the retort that threatened to spring out of his mouth. So now Katie was low-class, not polished enough for Dave's tastes? Dave, the small-minded jerk with barely average intelligence?

"And golf!" Dave laughed heartily. "Hell, she needs more help than ten pros could give her."

"No," Josh agreed slowly, "Katie's not good at golf."

His boss laughed again, the sound ugly and grating, no light of enjoyment in his eyes. "I'm not sure she's corporate wife material, son. Hell, she even encouraged Madison's nonsense about going back to school to be a social worker."

"Madison wants to go into social work?" Josh asked, trying to follow the breadcrumb trail of the older man's mental process. He was obviously steamed about something relating to Katie and it wasn't, apparently, anything to do with Josh's skipping out on the meeting.

The other man shrugged dismissively, contempt on his heavy countenance. "It's a silly impulse. Maddy's got a bee in her bonnet about going back to college. Stupid. I keep telling her she's got plenty on her hands. Getting a puny college degree like that won't enhance her best attributes."

So Dave's wife wanted a life of her own, Josh realized. And her husband felt threatened at the thought of not being the center of her universe.

"We've got a good life." Dave frowned, his expression shifting to a pout. "I give her everything she could possibly want. But seeing Katie working at that studio . . . following her dream, Maddy calls it . . . well, it's put some silly ideas in Maddy's head."

The picture snapped into focus in Josh's head.

"Then the fool girl goes and tells Maddy that social work is some kind of noble occupation," Dave jeered.

Yes, now he understood. Josh looked across the desk at the other man, noticing the faintest glimmer of fear in his eyes. It was pathetic, really, to see such a successful man so threatened by the thought of his wife earning accomplishments on her own. Apparently any achievement on her part offered Dave too much competition.

How ironic. With classic Flanagan flair, Katie had bumped up against Dave's most sensitive vulnerability.

Josh didn't bother trying to minimize this. Few people could be more dangerous than a weak man in a position of power. Unfortunately, the power he wielded directly impacted Josh's future.

"But it's nothing serious," Dave blustered, getting up. "I straightened Maddy out. Absolutely no college."

It might have done him good, but Josh couldn't bring himself to congratulate the ass on intimidating his own wife.

"The point is," Dave said, pausing in the act of opening the office door, "Katie doesn't fit."

Josh hated himself for the sinking feeling in his gut.

"I'm not sure your engagement is helping you. Think about it," his boss said meaningfully before he opened the door and left.

Staring at the empty doorway, Josh knew he was looking crisis in the face. Despite his personal dislike of the guy, Dave's support was vital to his getting the promotion.

He got up and closed his door, his hand shaking as he let the doorknob click back. Everything he wanted was so close, he could see it. Could imagine the solid sense of security that would snap into place around him.

He wasn't stupid enough to think himself invulnerable at that level, of course. Executives got the axe these days. But with the hefty salary and stock options that came with the job title, he'd have had enough, at last, to keep from having to worry. Enough to carry him to the next job.

If he got the promotion, he would accrue a cushion against the bumps ahead.

Walking back to his desk, he sat down and made himself think clearly. Katie couldn't keep her mouth shut, damn her. She'd given Dave's wife some advice that had angered the older man. But Josh wasn't giving up yet. He was not beaten yet. Pushing aside the rage that threatened at the thought of Dave's egotistic wimpiness, Josh considered his options.

He'd been a damned idiot for relying on Katie Flanagan! Hell, the woman had tampered with his boss's marriage! His *boss,* of all people! What the hell had she been thinking?

But this was no time to lose his grip, he reminded

himself. He shut out his surging fury. There was no way he was going to lose sight of the goal. Not when he'd come so close.

Forcing himself to relax against the chairback, the thought that business consultants didn't have to deal with this kind of crap flashed through Josh's mind. Didn't have to constantly find a way to stay on the boss's good side. They had to deal with politics, yes. Had to socialize. But there wasn't this daily threat, this constant compromising of their own values.

But then again, men like Dave could afford to be unfair. They'd attained that level in the company. The level Josh wanted.

And consultants also lived roller-coaster lives financially. Yes, he had a reputation in the company, had built respect with a certain number of people in the industry. But the big money—the perks, the stock deals, being able to retire in his fifties—all that was bought here, dealing with men like Dave.

He felt his anger subsiding, shrinking down and slinking back into the cage he'd learned to construct for his frustration. He'd always known the reality of this kind of business and had long ago made his choices. And his plans had been going great.

Till Katie Flanagan opened her luscious, talented mouth and put both feet inside. Put his career at risk.

He knew she'd done it unintentionally. Her soft heart and her heedless mouth. She wasn't Erin by a long shot; not mean-spirited or without loyalty. But she wasn't the woman to handle this kind of power over his career, either.

How could he have relied on so shaky a cohort?

Veering mentally away from Dave's assessment of her,

Josh made himself look at her with cold, dispassionate eyes. She was undeniably good in bed. That description didn't come close to how he felt when he was with her. She made him laugh, but it had been foolishness to think of having anything more with Katie.

Damn him, Dave was right about her not fitting in.

Josh wondered how he could have been so stupid to have lost himself in her drugging warmth, her sweet smiles and her infectious laughter. He'd been down the Flanagan road before—never so pleasantly, never with so little malice—but he wasn't a man to repeat his mistakes.

Picking up the phone, he punched in her number.

No way was he dumping her altogether. Dave couldn't be allowed to think he had that much power. Josh might have to dance to the boss's tune in some things, but this wouldn't be one of them. Not yet. Getting Katie in line without cutting her out of the picture might be tricky, but she undoubtedly had to stay involved if he wasn't to look like a bigger brownnoser than he felt.

With the studio phone ringing in his ear, Josh steeled himself to hear her soft voice. He might be stuck with her limited assistance until the promotion was done, but anything more . . . emotional wasn't a good idea.

Katie raced to pick up the phone, saying breathlessly into the receiver, "Flanagan's Photography. May I help you?"

"Katie?"

At the sound of his voice, she felt her insides melt.

"Josh! Good morning! Did you sleep well?"

"Fine," he said abruptly. "But I have some work here that needs finishing and I'm not going to make dinner."

"Oh," she said, her mood immediately deflating. "You know what we said about all work and no play—"

"Listen," he interrupted as if he hadn't heard her teasing remark. "Have you talked with Madison Williams recently?"

"No." Katie frowned at the curt note in his voice.

"Well, don't."

"Excuse me?" She took the receiver away from her ear briefly, glaring at it as if Josh could actually see her cutting stare.

"Don't talk with her until I have the opportunity to clue you in on some things," he ordered as if she were his lackey.

"Clue me in?" she sputtered in angry disbelief. "Why don't you take a second and do it now, hotshot?"

"I don't have time."

"Take the time!" What the heck had turned him into such a grouch, she wondered, not tolerating his lousy mood.

Katie could almost hear the annoyed quality of his pause.

"Fine. Apparently, Madison interpreted whatever you said to her about following your studio dream as encouragement to go back to college."

"Okay. So what if she did?" *This* was what had changed prince charming to a toad? "Why should you care?"

Josh's heavy sigh filtered through the phone line. "Look, I know the business world is foreign to you and that whatever you said, you didn't mean any harm—"

"What I said? All I said was that social workers are decent, worthwhile people!"

"I know," he responded, the weary, cynical note in his voice even more pronounced. "But she already has a career—as Dave Williams's wife. It pays well and it can't be done part-time."

"You've got to be kidding me!" Katie declared in outraged disbelief. "You mean that scummy husband of hers won't—

"Try to remember," Josh cut in, his voice tight, "that her husband—and I'm not arguing the scummy label—is the man who's my big hitter on this promotion."

"What does that have to do with anything?" she said in exasperation.

"Quite a lot." His anger receded again into that tired sound that made her want to cry. "I know you don't understand, Katie. But there are rules in the corporate world that have to be followed. One of them is never mess with your boss's wife and, by extension, never encourage your boss's wife to do something that scares the hell out of him. Unless you want to find yourself back in the mail room, that is."

"Good grief," Katie whispered, her words shaken. "He's *threatening* you over something I encouraged his wife to do?"

"Not in so many words," Josh said dryly. "But the meaning was very clear."

"My God." She felt the prickle of tears in her throat. What an ugly world to live in. "I'm sorry, Josh. It never occurred to me that my suggesting Madison go back to school could be used against you."

"I know," he said gently, his tone chillingly distant.

"Don't worry. I'm handling it, but I'd prefer you not talk to Madison right now."

"All right." Katie's hand felt numb, she was holding the phone so tightly.

"I'll call and let you know when I'll need you again."

He'd let her know when he would need her again?

"Okay. Good-bye." She hung up and stood next to the studio reception desk, staring down at the telephone.

"What's up?" Bethany leaned in the archway to the studio, one hand raised to hold back the curtain. "Problems with the fiancé?"

Glancing up, Katie said bluntly, "I'm in love with him."

Her friend paused, studying her face a moment. "Oh. And that's a bad thing?"

"Yes," Katie said slowly. "I don't know whether or not he cares for me at all. He's confused about things. He really thinks money and success are the most important goals."

Bethany held the curtain as Katie passed through the arch, going back into the studio where she'd been working before Josh's call. Blissfully working, happy in the memory of their idyllic afternoon together, in the sense of connection between them.

"Well," her friend said, climbing back up on the stool from which she'd been watching Katie's work. "I can see how having a boyfriend who thinks money and work come first might really suck. You'll never be first in his book."

"It's more than that," Katie said, the lump in her throat making the words painful. "At heart, Josh is this true-blue, honest-as-the-day-is-long guy. The kind who reports every cent on his income tax return and never calls in sick even when he is. A man who'd offer a pregnant woman the protection of his name even if he wasn't in love with her."

"Gee," Bethany drawled, adjusting herself on the stool, "the guy sounds like a Mountie."

"Better," Katie replied softly.

"A Mountie with a bank account?" Bethany grinned.

Too troubled to see the humor, Katie shook her head. "It's going to kill him."

Bethany stared at her. "The bank account or the Mountie thing?"

"Both, I guess." Katie sighed. "He wants to get this promotion at work. You know, the one I'm pretending to be his fiancée for?"

"Oh, yeah." Her friend lifted a brow. "Kind of veering from the straight and narrow path of truth for that promotion, isn't he?"

"Exactly." Katie sank onto a nearby footstool. She felt like crying. "He's playing games that aren't him. Doing things that go against his basic nature."

"Why?"

"He thinks he has to," Katie answered. "His parents died when he and his brother were young—actually left them destitute. I think he's determined to be secure financially, no matter what the cost."

"So he compromises his integrity for job success," Bethany concluded dispassionately.

"Yes, and he tells himself that's all he needs."

"He doesn't need you?" her friend guessed.

"Or anyone," Katie told her, propping her chin on top of her upraised fist. "He works all the time. Get this. He's the most attractive man I've ever known—"

"Indeed he is," Bethany averred.

"—and he's having to have a woman *pretend* to be engaged to him," Katie concluded sadly.

"But you've fallen in love with him."

"Yes."

"So, maybe after the promotion, he'll . . . ," Bethany's optimistic moment petered out.

"No," Katie said, easily finishing her friend's thought. "I don't think we have a future. I don't fit into the corporate climate and there's no room in his life for anything but his pursuit of security."

"Then you'd better cut loose," her friend advised practically. "The sooner the better."

"I know," Katie acknowledged, fighting the clog of tears in her throat, "but I can't."

"Listen, kid," Bethany said. "You've got to develop some self-preservation."

Katie shook her head. "I can't cut loose yet. I know he's way off course and sinking fast. I know he won't listen to anything I say, but I can't leave him. Not yet."

"When will you?" Bethany's face reflected more than her ordinary measure of skepticism.

"I don't know." Katie sighed again. "When he gets the darn promotion, I guess. When he's where he thinks he wants to be."

"Sounds risky to me," Bethany drawled.

"I know." How could she refute her friend's assessment when it was so glaringly accurate? "But I gave Josh my word that I wouldn't bail out on him, that I'd stay in until this is settled."

Bethany looked at her with compassionate eyes, but said nothing.

"If there's one thing I've learned from Josh," Katie said,

summoning up a tremulous smile, "it's that following through on promises can sometimes bring unexpected rewards. Even if it's just a sense of satisfaction."

Brushing at a trail of dampness on her cheek, she swallowed back the tears. "I have to do this. I can't . . . leave him until he's . . . okay."

Eleven

"Congratulations, Morgan," Dave Williams said, clapping Josh on the back again.

"You're the best person for the job," Adam Parker said, his gray hair lit by the windows spanning two walls of his office. He sat behind the huge slab of his mahogany desk with the complete assurance of a man who'd led three different companies to phenomenal success.

"Thank you, sir," Josh said, automatically rising to his feet to shake the hand offered him. This was it. The promotion to vice president in charge of production was his.

He'd fought for this moment so long and hard, dreamed about it. And now here it was, the big boss offering him his shot at the future he'd worked for. "I'll do my best, sir."

"We know you will," Parker rose to his feet, signaling the end of the interview. "As I said, you have a good performance record with the company and high recommendations from your superiors. I think we'll all be happy with this move."

"I can assure you I am," Josh said with a smile.

"Well, good." Adam Parker looked down at the papers on his desk as if his mind had already left their conversation. "My assistant will show you which office will be yours."

"Thank you," he said again, turning to leave.

Beside him, Dave Williams hesitated, saying in his too-jovial way, "Adam, we still on for those eighteen holes on Friday?"

Parker glanced up, a brief smile creasing his face as he picked up his phone. "Yes, of course."

"Good. Good," Dave responded, following Josh out of the office.

Pausing at the desk of Adam Parker's assistant, situated a few steps outside of his office, Josh ascertained his own office assignment. He was aware of Dave lingering at his elbow.

"I appreciate it," Josh told the assistant when she handed him the key to his new office. "I'll probably get moved in this weekend."

"That's the way," Dave said as they moved away from the assistant's desk and headed for the elevators. "Jump in with both feet and hit the ground running. That's what I like about you. You're dedicated."

"Thanks," Josh said, tired of repeating the word, but aware that it behooved him to keep his allies.

"This is quite a step for you," Williams commented as they traversed a long hall.

"Yes. I'm very grateful for the opportunity." Josh arrived at the bank of elevators and punched the down button.

"Quite a step," the other man repeated. "I've known a lot of men who took ten years to get where you've gotten in five."

Josh realized why Dave was still beside him. He wanted

acknowledgement. Wanted a display of appreciation and gratitude for what he saw as his part in Josh's success. It was nothing more than any boss would expect when an employee was promoted.

But the words stuck in Josh's throat. He'd worked his tail off for this company and had done a good job in spite of the pompous ass standing next to him. If anything, Williams had been a hindrance to his success. But telling the man that would earn Josh an implacable enemy, and even though Dave no longer had any direct power over him, they still had to work together.

The elevator door slid open as Josh was forming the words he knew had to be said.

"I appreciate your assistance in my getting this job," he said when the two had stepped into the elevator car and turned to face the numbers. "I know you were a big part of my getting the promotion."

Williams's chest seemed to swell. "Well, Parker asked me about your job performance and your commitment."

He paused, sliding Josh a significant glance.

Keeping his attention on the door, Josh's thoughts flickered to the other man's anger over Katie encouraging his wife's ambitions. It wasn't a thing Dave would forget easily.

"When I answered him," Dave continued, "I thought back over your time with the company. For the most part, you have a good work ethic. Don't mind staying till the job's done. Never whined about having to travel at the last minute."

Josh shrugged. "Sometimes it has to be done."

"Exactly my point," Williams said smugly. "I think you basically have what it takes to do the job."

"Thanks," Josh said again, the word beginning to feel like it came from some remote, mechanical part of himself.

To his relief, the elevator came to a stop and the doors slid open.

"Yes, sir," Dave said heartily, slapping him on the back again. "You'll figure out what's important. In no time, you'll be fitting in just like the rest of us."

Watching his former boss leave the elevator, Josh had no trouble interpreting Dave's last remark, though it took him a moment to shake the chill from the idea of "fitting in" like Dave.

He knew what the other man referred to. Katie. His supposed fiancée. She didn't fit in, she'd overstepped her boundaries and in doing so, irritated his boss. But in spite of that, Josh had still gotten the promotion. His hard work had won out over that one major mistake.

Alone in the elevator now, he reflected on the significance of the last half hour. This was it. He'd reached his goal. Made it to the top. His moment of attainment. But now that it had arrived, he felt oddly detached. Unquestionably, there was a sense of accomplishment. Of validation. He'd earned it. He'd known he could do this job if given a chance. And now some fairly astute business minds appeared to concur with him on that.

He couldn't deny the sense of satisfaction in that, but along with it came the knowledge that he had to make sure he justified their faith in him. Of course, the transition period between positions would entail hard work. He'd have to find his feet quickly.

But he knew how to work hard. It was nothing new. He'd worked five hard years to get to this point.

Your work is never done. Katie's voice floated through his mind as the elevator stopped again, this time on his floor.

Katie, he thought, stepping out of the elevator door and turning down the hall to his office. The job was his now. He didn't actually need Katie to pretend to be his fiancée anymore.

Yes, he'd still have to play the old boys's game, and that involved having a sexually attractive woman on his arm at all business social functions. But it didn't have to be Katie.

The thought of squiring some other faceless woman left him unexcited, but that didn't change the reality.

In truth, it would do him no harm in his work circle for it to seem that he'd dumped Katie. He'd only asked her to commit to this charade until the job was his. And she'd stuck it out, amazingly, even when things had gotten rough. He hadn't really expected that of her.

He walked down the corridor, suddenly assailed by the memory of her soft lips opened beneath his, her delectable body naked in his arms. Instant heat streaked through him.

Glancing at the open office area he was passing through, he knew he had to change his thoughts or run the risk of seeming way too excited about work.

Slipping past his secretary and shutting his office door, Josh sat down in his desk chair and stared into space.

He hadn't seen Katie for a week, since their afternoon interlude—a week since he'd lost himself in her hot, sweet passion and lain next to her in her sweet-smelling bed and laughed at her playful silliness.

It had been a damn long week, but he'd made himself go without seeing her just to prove to himself that he hadn't stupidly let her crawl under his skin. Getting hooked on Katie made no sense at all. It wasn't just her Flanagan blunder with Dave's wife. That had just been a reminder to Josh of the essential reasons why he had to step carefully.

It would be insanity to let Katie worm her way into his heart. She *didn't* know the rules of corporate life and he suspected she didn't want to know them. Hell, Katie lived life by her own rules, if any.

Even if she had stuck out the term of her agreement with him, she still wasn't reliable. She wasn't the steadfast, dependable woman he would eventually marry.

Any way he looked at it, Katie wasn't the woman for him. If they developed a relationship, she would refuse to respect his work time and refuse to understand why it was so important to him.

But Josh still wanted her.

He sat back in his chair and remembered lying in the grass kissing her. Remembered her beautiful, laughing face. The breathless giddiness she brought to him. Surely there was no reason to give that up yet. He didn't have to give up the heat and lust. They could be lovers a while longer. It wasn't as if he was using her against her will. She wanted him, too. She'd made that perfectly clear through her earth-shattering response to him.

Drawing a deep breath, he released it slowly, his mind made up. The six-month period they'd set to give her a chance to make a go of the studio wasn't up. He could give himself that length of time to revel in the fabulous commotion of her sexuality.

He could be with her, for that long anyway, without endangering either his future or his heart too much.

* * *

Two hours later, Josh glanced at his watch and wondered what Katie was doing for lunch. If he left the office now, he could stop by the studio.

The studio with the big satin bed on its raised platform.

Shutting down his computer, he grabbed his suit coat from the back of his chair and left his office.

The drive to Flanagan's Photography took him less than ten minutes. Josh parked in the potholed parking lot, noting that only Katie's beat-up MG sat outside the building. She was here and she was alone.

Walking quickly up to the front door of the pink stucco building, he felt his pulse quicken and pushed away the niggling sense of conscience. He'd never forced her to be with him physically. That hadn't been any part of their agreement.

She wanted him just as he wanted her.

Opening the heavy glass door, Josh stepped into the building and stopped, allowing his eyes to adjust to the cool dimness of the reception area.

"Josh?"

Katie sat behind the front desk, the tumble of her red hair a bright contrast to the drab surroundings.

"I've been thinking about you," he blurted out and then stopped, appalled at his own lack of finesse.

She smiled, a hint of shyness on her vivid face. "Have you?"

"Yes," he acknowledged, searching urgently to find some suavity to smooth out the sudden rush of need and longing he felt for her. Searching and finding none.

"Are you alone? Are you expecting anyone?"

She rose to her feet, a sudden hint of a flush in her cheeks. "I'm alone. I don't have anyone scheduled for an hour."

The breathlessness in her voice and the way she stood there, hesitation and longing in her face, encouraged Josh to go with the urgency thundering in his own veins. Reaching back, he flipped the lock on the door.

When he turned back to where she stood, one hand resting against the desk, he saw her eyes wide, her face flooded with the same tremulous anticipation he felt. For one fragile instant, they looked at each other and then he had her in his arms, her slender body pressed to his.

"I've missed you," he said roughly, not caring that it was the last thing he should have said, the worst thing to feel for her, of all women.

"Josh," she said, breathing his name like a prayer.

Lowering his mouth to hers, he met her eager kiss and lost his head. She smelled sweet and heady, her body soft against his in ways that haunted his dreams. Yet he felt the strength of her arms around him, felt the hot dueling of her tongue against his.

She was heat; warmth; sultry nights; sunlit days; a heady, drunken spell he couldn't fight. If he could only take her, lay claim to her body a few more times . . . Not more than a hundred. Then he maybe he could cure himself of the yearning.

Scooping Katie up into his arms, he turned and brushed through the curtained archway into the studio. Curling into his arms as if she were made for him to carry, she laid her head on his shoulder and threaded her fingers into his hair.

Josh slowed down his step, crossing the studio with her

in his arms until he stood next to her satin bed. Strangely reluctant to release her, he bent his head to hers and kissed her slowly. Long and poignant they kissed, his heart thundering in his chest. She was light in his arms, the skin of her legs firm where he held her.

Gently lowering her legs so she could stand beside him, he held their kiss. Even as he felt her hands dragging at his shirt buttons, tugging at his belt, still he kissed her, his hands braced lightly at her back.

No blundering rush to completion would do. He wanted to sink slowly into her damp heat, wanted to hear her cry out in release, over and over. He'd been celibate for a week, a long, hungry week, and he felt his own arousal clawing at him. But this enchantment of her firm breasts in his hands, the pouting nipples pressing into his palms—he had to savor this. Had to draw her smooth, silky body against his harder, rougher flesh and relish their diversity.

With all the treasure of Katie in his hands, how could he rush? How could he want it to be over too soon?

Lying her back against the silken coverlet moments later, he stood next to the bed naked and devoured her with his hot gaze. Her red-gold hair tumbled against the gleaming satin, a shiny tangle of fire; flames against the ivory of her shoulders, her breasts.

She lifted her arms to him, drawing him onto the bed beside her. Kneeling there, he bent and took one luscious nipple into his mouth, swirling his tongue over her, absorbing her taste, her smell. Her cries of pleasure, of encouragement left him flushed, harder than iron but determined to make their loving leisurely.

He smoothed his palm over her rib cage, down over her silken-smooth tummy to the crisp fire between her legs.

He found her damp crevices and let his fingers wander there in the magical folds. Moments later, Katie stiffened and cried out, her hands clutching at him.

Josh felt his heart jerk in his chest at the sound of her sobbing release, his name on her lips.

Lying down beside her, her body still shuddering, he cradled her hip with the flat of his hand. With his face buried in the curve of her neck, he nipped at her creamy skin and braced her slender shoulders so that she lay on her side facing him. Her breasts were breathtakingly full against his chest, her smooth leg curved over his body.

Nudging forward, he probed at her damp cleft and with one thrust, slid home. Lying on their sides, face-to-face, he stroked into her, his hands free to toy with her breasts.

Her eyes were wide open, a startling glitter of blue in her flushed face. The "O" of her parted lips was damp and pink. He loved the way she held him, her hands tight at his waist, her leg thrown over him, curling behind his buttocks to urge him forward. Closer, deeper.

Smooth and slow, he entered and withdrew, sharply attuned to the rising tide of need in his body, the urgency pounding against his skin. He heard her quickened breathing, saw the glazing over of her eyes as their bodies moved together; then, the catch of her breath as her head rolled back, the tightening of her body around his as she cried out, her body constricting his in a way that threatened a beautiful madness. Lowering his hand to the small of her back, Josh drove into her, bracing her against the force of his urgency, the completion that could not be denied any longer.

"Oh, God, Josh!" she cried out, meeting his thrusts

with her own desperate frenzy, her own shattering response.

He drove into her over and over until his breath deserted him and all he could do was hold her against his body while the fire consumed them.

Lying with her limp in his arms, he fought to draw in a breath and listened to the thunder of blood against his eardrums. Being with her tore him out of this world and hurtled him into some other place, a place of sensation and wonderment, of complete connection.

He drifted back to earth, very slowly, his arms still full of luscious naked Katie and his clearing head fighting a sense of utter dismay.

He didn't want to tell her about the promotion, didn't want anything to shift the delicate balance that brought them here to this blissful unity. For the first time in his life, he wanted to lie to a woman, to connive and manipulate. Wanted to do whatever had to be done to keep her here, compliant and warm in his heart.

He'd had so little in life in the way of emotional fulfillment. Didn't he deserve to keep this part of Katie to himself? She didn't have to be a part of his other world. Couldn't he find a way to construct a private place in his life? Even if he found some other woman to be his corporate escort, couldn't he still keep Katie—just this warm, joyful, loving part—for himself?

Angrily, Josh drew her relaxed body closer.

Unreliable, flighty, inconsistent, inappropriate Katie. A Flanagan to the core. Why couldn't he keep her in the dark as long as possible? He'd come to her when he couldn't resist any longer and he'd make love to her like this, until they were both utterly spent. She didn't stay with anything or anyone very long, but wouldn't this be worth lying for, as long as he could get away with it?

As long as she didn't know about his new job, he had a chance of making love to her, of keeping things status quo.

"Katie!" Josh said abruptly. "I got the promotion today."

Now was the hard part, Katie said to herself later that afternoon as she approached Josh's office. Now she had to leave him.

Sara Harper must have been on a hypoglycemic snack break, since her desk was empty. Lifting her hand, Katie knocked on the door.

"Come in," Josh called.

She opened the door and went in.

"Katie!"

"Hi." She closed the door behind her and stood uncertainly beside the chair in front of his desk. It seemed fitting to end the relationship here where she'd started it blindly so many weeks ago. She had to get through this without crying.

Josh came around his desk and dropped a hard kiss on her surprised mouth. "Did your session go well? Client show up?"

"Yes," she said awkwardly, feeling the warmth steal into her cheeks at the reminder of their passionate lunch interlude. Truthfully, she'd had no time then to respond to his bombshell announcement about the promotion. With her next photography client due within a few minutes,

Katie had had to get dressed, straighten the studio and lose the naked man before the woman arrived.

The timing hadn't been so bad, though, she reflected sadly, still standing next to the chair as he returned to his place behind his desk. She'd needed to think some things through, needed to gird herself for this conversation.

"I want to talk to you," she said now, clearing her throat and struggling to keep her voice level.

"Of course. Sit down," Josh told her, a small frown gathering on his forehead in response, she knew, to her serious tone.

Stepping around to sit down, she caught the glance he sent flashing over her clothes. Electric blue capri pants and a sleeveless tropical print shirt. Comfort apparel and something more, she knew. She'd dressed this way to underscore the difference between who she was and who he had been requiring her to be. No more corporate drone.

Unquestionably, she didn't fit into his chosen world. If the truth were told, he probably saw her as threatening his safe existence. Only with his body did he trust her, not with his emotions, his heart. Never had he given her that, she thought, the pain of that fact slicing into her. She knew he considered her unworthy of his faith.

Today after a week apart, he'd come to join with her body, for sex. Nothing more. She felt her own heart leave her at his slightest touch, but to him their lovemaking meant only physical release. Ever since he'd left her this afternoon, she'd been working to make herself accept that fact. Every part of her wanted to cling to him, wanted to shy away from the pain of never seeing him again. But she knew she'd be selling her soul for a small sliver of the dream.

"So," he said, a guarded expression in his eyes, "what's up?"

Katie looked at him, trying to keep the bleakness off her face. She cleared her throat again and said bluntly, "Now that you have your promotion, there's no need for us to continue pretending."

He looked at her for a long moment. "Pretending."

"The corporate fiancée thing," she said around the hard lump in her throat. This was hard enough without his playing dumb. She didn't want to leave him, didn't want to give up his kisses and the hope that one day he'd give her his love along with his body. But she was determined not to be a fool anymore. There was a limit to how much abuse one heart could take.

"Okay," he said after a pause, "if that's how you want it. You don't have to bother anymore with my office stuff."

Katie watched him sadly, seeing the flicker of relief in his eyes. After the thing with Madison, she must be as much a liability to his career as anything else.

"Okay," she said, still trying to steady her voice. "Well, I'll start making the loan payments next month. Maybe we'll run into one another sometime."

Josh's brows snapped together, his smile vanishing. "Just because you're not pretending to be my fiancée doesn't mean we can't see one another."

"Why?" she asked him painfully, meeting his gaze across the desk. "There's no future in it. I'm not corporate wife material and I upset your boss."

"This has nothing to do with him," Josh snapped irritably. "We can date. It's no one's business who I see outside of work."

Katie looked at him, stunned by the irony of his statement. From the beginning, he'd "seen" her expressly for his work. Now that she was a liability, he'd keep his involvement with her hidden away. So he'd see her—have sex with her—but find another escort for the business events, she realized with a surge of anger. He wanted a covert sexual relationship.

"I don't think so," she said finally, succumbing to the angry urge to push him into an admission. "Why would we do that? What reason would we have?"

Annoyance flared on his face. "If this afternoon is anything to go by, we both have some damn good reasons to continue seeing each other. By my count, you had three *reasons.*"

Katie felt the heat flame up in her face. The bastard. She might have known he'd try and use the sex against her.

"No," she said baldly, jerking to her feet to glare at him across the desk. "I'm not having a secret sexual relationship with you."

"Don't talk like we're cheating on anyone," he demanded. "We're both free agents. Whose business is it if we sleep together?"

Trying to still the trembling sickness in her stomach, Katie said with effort, "Look, you don't get it. It's not just sex for me. I . . . care for you, but you can't trust me with your heart. You've given it to this corporate world. Sold yourself for—"

"You're dumping me. Bailing out again," he rapped out furiously, not responding to her halting admission of love. "This isn't about my work. What kind of fool do you take me for? Getting men to trust you with their heart is a pattern with you. This is just another fling for you, isn't it? Your other *fiancés* trusted you and where did it get them?"

"It is about your work! You're obsessed," she said, lifting a hand in a half plea. "Fearful and terrified of not making a success in this world. It's all-consuming. I know you had a terrible childhood—"

"That's ridiculous," he thundered, on his feet as well, the two of them facing off across the battlefield. "My childhood has nothing to do with why you're refusing to see me."

"Okay," Katie said, giving up before she broke down and wept. "Believe what you want."

"So that's it? You're just walking away?"

Katie was half turned blindly toward the door when Josh's demand stopped her.

"What else can I do?" she asked him passionately.

"The six months aren't up!" he yelled. "And you're bailing again. Running out!"

"No," she said, "I'm going to run the studio and pay my bills—"

"So it's just *me* you're running out on," he accused furiously.

"No!" Her breath came hard in her throat, tears stung at the back of her eyes. "I did my part. You got your damn promotion. The game is over."

"Yes," he sneered, his beautiful face taut with ugly anger. "And you got quite a lot out of our game, didn't you. Aside from the obvious physical rewards."

"What are you talking about?" she demanded, her heart breaking.

"You. Riding on my coattails," he told her, his face drawn into a snarl. "Using my connections to get your damn studio started. Who introduced you to Madison Williams? Me! Who got you the women's club contract? Madison."

"Don't be stupid," Katie retorted furiously, fighting to keep from slapping his incensed face. "I've worked hard for this. I may have met Madison through you, but *my* work and *my* portfolio got me the job!"

"Don't you wish!" Josh mocked. "Madison knew me, her husband knew me. Do you think they'd have had anything to do with your shabby little business if they hadn't known me? That's how business works. *All* business."

"It's sad if you believe that," Katie yelled at him, so mad she could barely think. "You've sold yourself for *business*. Sold your integrity for this job. For the security you so desperately need. And if you stay here, you'll lose your soul, too."

"What are you babbling about?" He stared at her in hostile disbelief.

"Look at what this job is doing to you! You're honest and dependable and steadfast. And look at the way you're living," she demanded furiously. "You did things to earn this promotion that went against your basic character!"

"That's ridiculous."

"Oh, so you normally lie to your friends and coworkers and tell them you're *engaged* to women who you're not even involved with? Do you normally suck up to people you don't respect?"

"Shut up!" Josh glared at her. "I've earned this job, worked my ass off for it."

"But that's not why they gave it to you!" she yelled. "It's because you play golf! Because you keep your real feelings to yourself! Because you can *play the game!*"

"Everything in life worth having requires some sacrifice," he said, his words tight, his eyes dark with rage.

"No!" Katie drew in a sobbing breath. "Not this much sacrifice. Not betrayal of your true nature every single day of your life."

Josh stared at her across the desk, his face a stiff mask.

She brushed angrily at the tears coursing down her face. "You may choose to live like this, selling yourself for your security, but I'm not staying here to watch it."

Turning on her heel, Katie ran out of his office.

Twelve

Josh sank into his desk chair and settled his trembling hands on the solid surface in front of him. His ears rang with Katie's words, the din mingling with the cacophony of his own thundering heartbeat.

His chest felt tight, his lungs constricted, and for a moment, he wondered if this was what a heart attack felt like. This crushing pain and blurring of vision. What had she said? That he'd end up losing his soul along with his integrity?

Maybe he was having an integrity attack. Perhaps that was what left him gasping, left a burning sandpaper feel to his eyes.

Only this morning, he'd taken her into his arms and loved them both into satiated oblivion. How could a thing turn ugly so soon after that? Hadn't he shown her his tenderness? Loved her with all the tangled mess of feelings he couldn't even define for himself?

He winced. God. The things he'd said to her just now.

Sinking his head onto his hands, Josh suffered the memory of his own words. Had he really claimed total responsibility for her successes? Accused her of using him for gain and then dumping her? It wasn't true and he hadn't meant it. Katie had worked hard in the last six weeks, far harder than he'd ever expected, and the studio's increasing business was due to her follow-through.

Katie Flanagan stuck it out and made a success of so unlikely a venture. Incredible. Or maybe not. Maybe she'd always had it in her and he just hadn't seen it.

Getting up from his desk, Josh went to close his office door, still flung open from when Katie had rushed out. He glanced into his secretary's office, profoundly grateful to find it empty. No one had heard them and the way he'd yelled at her. He wasn't proud of how he'd handled Katie's farewell.

He surely didn't want anyone to hear him yelling about the sacrifices he'd made for his promotion. He was selling himself, Katie had said. Josh shook his head in an attempt to clear it. She didn't understand how this world worked. He was just playing the game everyone else played. A man could stand on his integrity when he wasn't shooting for the stars, but making the big time required tact. He hadn't really been sucking up to Dave Williams and the others above him. He was just using diplomacy.

But that little nuance of distinction didn't change the fact that she was gone.

She left him, and his bitter accusations and his condemning, terrified attempts to make her stay. What a fool he'd been, and undoubtedly still was.

Closing the door quietly, he leaned against it, swamped by a sudden wave of loss and grief. Gone. She'd come to him out of the blue six weeks before, disrupting his careful world. And she'd brought fireworks and laughter to his days, warmth and a piercing sense of connection that scared the hell out of him.

God, the life she'd brought to him.

Only now she'd left. Abandoned him back into the dark well of his daily existence, the heavy grind of his weeks. No Katie. No hot kisses or surprise picnics.

What did she want of him? Promises? Lies? She'd said the corporate world was going to steal his soul, but he couldn't envision leaving it, this world he'd scrambled long and hard to succeed in. And he wasn't doing anything so different than a thousand other guys did everyday.

It was life in this modern world, as bitter as the requirements sometimes were.

Returning to his desk, Josh stared at his blank computer monitor, unable to summon any interest in the things he knew he had to finish up before the week was out. It was insane, after winning his promotion, to feel so bereft. So lost.

If only he hadn't been such an ass with Katie, maybe he could have pointed out to her the benefits of maintaining their relationship the way it was. Maybe he could have found the words to give her what she wanted. She'd said she cared for him.

Josh rubbed at the throbbing spot between his brows, feeling as though she'd blown a hole in his chest.

He was abandoned again. But didn't he deserve it this time?

From the first, he'd known she couldn't fit into his world, that asking her to do so would be unfair to them both. But it had seemed like such a lovely solution to both his problem and hers, such a tempting proposition with Katie being the dazzling bauble that drew his lusting thoughts.

Leaning forward decisively, Josh turned on the computer. What was done, was done. No matter how painful, how unbearable it seemed, he still had to function, still had to move forward. After all, he'd reached a major goal in his life, as tarnished as that goal might be in some people's eyes.

If he felt like all his internal organs were failing him, so what? There was always work and more work.

Katie leaned the ladder against the stucco exterior of the studio. Picking up her paint roller and bucket, she climbed up and began painting where she'd left off.

In the two weeks since she'd broken things off with Josh, she'd gone on a rampage. Cleaning all the junk out of the studio's two storerooms she'd kept only usable costumes and props. She'd also put up new curtains and painted most of the exterior of the building, albeit the latter she was doing with Bethany's capable help.

And she'd missed him. Thought about him. Worried about him. Which was stupid. He had what he wanted now, what he'd always made his priority.

"You missed a spot," Bethany said from behind her, startling Katie so much she grabbed at the ladder to keep from falling.

Swiping the roller over the area again, Katie said, "It looks great, doesn't it?"

"Yes." Her friend leaned closer, examining her face. "Did you get any sleep last night?"

"Sure," Katie said, lying cheerfully. The nights were a hell of longing and despair, but she wasn't giving in, wasn't losing sight of her progress here. Wasn't losing her mind.

"You've got the inside of this place looking terrific,

Bethany commented, the concerned look still in her eyes. "You must be working like a dog."

"Just getting things done," Katie declared, pushing the paint roller hard against the stucco to get the pigment into all the crevices of the rough surface.

"Well, I'm all for being productive," Bethany drawled as she washed her brush at the nearby water faucet, "but this burst of activity seems suspiciously aberrant to me. Are you sure you're all right with this Josh thing?"

"Don't be ridiculous," Katie scoffed, stretching her mouth into a wide smile. "I'm fine."

Bethany looked at her a long moment. "I hope so."

"Never been better," Katie claimed, taking a last swipe at the wall. "There. All done."

Drying her brush on a clean rag, Bethany surveyed the finished project. "It's a good thing this place isn't larger. I was starting to develop a liking for the smell of latex paint."

"It looks terrific." Katie climbed down the ladder, balancing her roller on the top of the open paint can.

"Very nice. Did you repaint the inside of the studio, too?"

"Yes." Keeping her face and voice bright all the time took effort, but it was almost becoming automatic to don her cheerfulness like she put on her shoes each morning.

"When did you do it?" her friend persisted. "I was here two days ago and I know you've been doing a lot of sittings."

Katie bent to rinse her roller. "I did it in the evenings."

"You mean the one evening before you started painting the outside?"

"Yes."

Bethany paused before pronouncing, "I'm worried about you, kid."

"Don't be." Katie rinsed the roller, her brain both numb and buzzing with random thoughts. She loved the studio, loved her work here, but being here so close to Josh was making her crazy. "Hey, I'm thinking about moving up to Minnesota and joining Erin's rock band. She says they're getting gigs all over the place and she wants me to join."

Bethany stared at her. "Have you lost your mind?"

"Of course not." Katie put the lid on the paint can, not looking at her friend. "It just sounds like fun and I haven't spent much time with Erin since she left—"

"Katie!" Bethany took her by the shoulders. "Katie, get a grip here. You don't play music and you don't much trust your sister. Listen, I know you love Josh and you're hurting, but don't do this. Don't give up this place. Don't give up your work!"

Katie's hyperkinetic brain stopped in midflow. She stared into her friend's worried face and felt her careful composure slipping. The world wavered before her eyes as they filled with tears, her face contorted as she let her facade slip.

Her knees buckled under her as she sank onto the last rung of the ladder, tears trickling down her cheeks.

"But it hurts so bad," she whispered, the words broken. "I feel like I'm going to die."

"I know," Bethany said, kneeling down to hug her close. "I know."

"So what you're telling me is all you want is for me to help you make Stevenson look bad?" Josh asked slowly.

Annoyance settled over Dave Williams's face. "I wouldn't put it that way, Morgan. It's just that this guy is on shaky ground because he can't handle the job. His unit is affecting everyone else, pulling the rest of us down."

"So you want my report to reflect even more badly on him?" Josh looked across his new desk, feeling strangely calm. In the month since he'd been given this job, he'd had the opportunity to see the game being played at a whole new level. The highest level of corporate deal-making.

Unfortunately, he didn't like the game any better.

"All I said was that you needed to stress the problems he's causing for production," Dave said with irritation. "But it's your report. Write it any way you want."

"Thanks."

"But you haven't been in this position very long," his former boss pointed out, an edge to his voice, "and you may not realize how important it is to put blame squarely where it belongs. If it's him or me, I'll vote for Stevenson's head on the chopping block."

"Naturally." He didn't think the other man even heard the irony in his voice.

"And in this company," Williams informed him meaningfully, "you have to make sure to take care of your friends."

Josh looked at Dave, thinking of the mean-spirited way he treated his employees, the contempt he demonstrated toward any coworker he didn't fear. *This* man was his friend?

Williams got up to leave. "Think about it."

Watching him go, Josh thought again about how much he disliked Dave Williams. Unfortunately, being promoted to the same level as the man didn't mean he had to deal with him any less often.

Behind Josh, sunlight streamed through the bank of windows that made up one wall of his new office, the light reflecting off the polished top of his larger desk. At least, the part not littered over with paper.

In the month that he'd had this job, he'd traveled three days out of every four. Albuquerque. Wilmington. Seattle. All of them a blur of meetings, cold hotel rooms and bad food.

No Katie to call on the phone. No Katie to come home to.

Only more hotel rooms in more strange cities, week after week. As a new manager, he'd had to make himself known to his production employees, had to familiarize himself with his people.

And the travel wasn't the hardest part, he was realizing.

Night after night, he kept hearing Katie's voice talking about his integrity, kept remembering her blue eyes swimming with tears. Every time he agreed with a proposition in a meeting put forth by another manager, he found himself wondering if he was being truthful or "tactful."

In the four long weeks of his short tenure, he'd been called on over and over again to endorse and support business practices in which he couldn't place his fullest confidence. Yet that was how business was conducted at this level. Almost like a politician, he had to keep the lines of communication open between himself and his own co-workers, not only for his own job's sake, but for his subordinates, the people counting on him. For them, he had to make compromises where he found himself tempted to hold firm.

Three times in the last four weeks, he'd also found himself calling Michael Topher, his former coworker. Of course, as a freelance consultant, Michael had a lot of industry information to offer. But to Josh's surprise, their last two conversations had been more about Michael's business than Josh's.

From Michael's information, the consulting business wasn't as unsteady as Josh had always thought.

Looking down now at the report he had been working on, he wondered when his disenchantment with his job had started. For so long, he'd worked toward gaining this level in the company and, over the years, he'd unconsciously counted on life improving when he reached upper management. He'd always told himself he'd have time for a family later, that he'd be able to relax a little when he got to this point.

Only here he was and he hadn't had a day of relaxation since he'd moved into this office. There was still no letting up, and there was certainly no room for a family. Not the way he wanted to raise kids, anyway.

The phone on his desk rang then.

"Josh Morgan speaking," he said into the receiver.

"Hey, how does it feel to be the big cheese?" Rick Goring asked, laughing.

"Hi, Rick." Josh leaned back in his chair.

"Say, buddy," his friend said, "now that you're so much above me, I find myself developing the urge to do you favors."

"Really? What a surprise," Josh said, a dry note in his voice.

"Yes," Rick agreed, chuckling. "I'm just a nice guy."

"Since when?"

Rick said jovially, "It's a personality trait that comes and goes."

"I'll say." Josh glanced down at the report that still needed to be finished. "So what favor are you feeling the urge to do for me?"

"I'll tell you," Rick said. "Since you've ended your arrangement with the beautiful and delicious Katie, I thought you might like a replacement."

"What are you talking about?" Josh asked, the words coming out with more snap than he'd intended.

"An accessory," Rick said, chiding. "I mean, you've got to wear someone on your arm at your big cheese events, and I've recently run across several prime candidates."

"No, thanks." The thought of dating another woman left him with a sick feeling in his gut.

"Are you sure? Think about it," Rick suggested, his tone wheedling. "These are some really lovely ladies and very presentable, if you know what I mean."

Josh did know and felt sickened by the inference. Sickened by the whole conversation, with its implications of procurement.

"Listen, Rick," he said with an effort. "I don't really have time right now—I don't need dates."

"Okay, fine," his friend said, laughing again. "But when you do, I'm the guy you call."

"Sure. Whatever. Hey, I'll give you a ring later," Josh said, resisting the urge to lambaste Rick for playing the game so damn well. "I'm in the middle of some things here and I really need to get back to work."

"Do that, buddy," Rick said. "We'll play golf."

Josh hung up the phone seconds later, aware of his palms sweating and his stomach having tightened into a knot.

God. As if he could replace Katie like a burned-out bulb on a string of Christmas lights. Simply remove her from his life and plug in the next woman.

In the space of an instant, Josh conjured Katie up in his mind. Katie to come home to, her lap filled with red-haired children. Irreplaceable Katie with her beautiful smile and her dancing eyes.

Josh stared blankly into the large office. He missed her so much, he physically ached. The nights were the worst. Time after time, he'd picked up the phone to call her. Surely she wouldn't reject him, wouldn't refuse to talk to him.

But every time, he'd put the phone down, remembering her words, her tears. Remembering her saying she couldn't watch him sell his soul for security.

Well, here he was. Secure. And lonely as hell.

"You're going back to school?" Katie hugged her friend across the studio reception desk. "Oh, Madison. How wonderful. But what about Dave? Isn't he upset?"

Madison leaned against the desk, a confident smile on her face. "He was, at first, but I just kept explaining to him how much better his life will be if I'm happy."

"True," Katie agreed, her friend's news brightening her own dismal mood. "This is wonderful. When do you start?"

"Next semester. I have to wait for my high school transcripts," she said, her smile faltering. "Oh, Katie, I'm terrified of the math and English. I wasn't a very good student in high school."

"Who was?" Katie grimaced. "But I know you'll do well now. It matters more to you."

"True," Madison agreed, her optimism returning.

"So, Katie," Susan Chapman said, stepping through the curtained archway from the studio, "when can I see my proofs?"

"In about a week—"

The recently installed bell on the studio door jangled then, drawing Katie's attention to the man who walked into the reception area.

The other two women turned as well, but she was hardly aware of them, her world narrowing, focusing on Josh as he stood in front of her. She registered his broad-shouldered form, the tieless white shirt open at the neck, and felt herself stiffening in shock.

"Josh!" His name came tumbling out of her mouth as a surge of longing, pain and love threatened to overwhelm her. She put a hand on the reception desk to steady her suddenly trembling legs.

He looked drawn, the tense expression in his eyes strangely vulnerable.

"I need to talk to you," he said with a complete lack of finesse, totally ignoring the two women standing next to the reception desk.

"Uh, hi, Josh," Madison said, her glance swinging between him and Katie. "Um, Susan, why don't we go into the studio."

"Sure," the older woman said, casting a last curious look their way as Madison led her through the curtained arch.

Katie and Josh stood facing each other, the chipped pink Formica counter between them. As the curtains in the archway swung shut, Katie stepped nervously around the reception desk, her trembling hand resting on the cool surface.

He was here, his face pale, his gaze hungry on her face; and she had to be strong. No matter how much she'd longed to be in his arms, how many nights she'd cried herself to sleep over him, she couldn't let herself be talked into a casual sexual relationship that would destroy her.

Never in her life had crumbs sounded so good. She would do anything to be with him, to hear his voice. Only she knew she couldn't. Couldn't for herself and, even more, for him.

Out of the corner of her eye, Katie saw the curtains in the archway move slightly and she realized the women on the other side could probably hear everything. But she didn't care. Josh was here and nothing else mattered.

"How are you?" she asked, her voice faint under the weight of her longing. She wanted to throw herself into his arms, to kiss his beautiful mouth and tell him she'd be whatever he wanted her to be.

But she knew she couldn't, so she just stood there, her gaze clinging to him with what she knew was a stupid longing.

"I've quit my job," he said without preamble.

A soft gasp filtered through the curtained archway through which Madison and Susan had gone.

"What?" For a moment, Katie wondered if she'd lost touch with reality.

"I quit," he repeated, his gaze intense on her face. "I've been in my new job, getting settled in, trying to be happy about it. Finally, I realized you were right. I've been losing chunks of myself, day after day, year after year. Negotiating and compromising my way through everything. Sacrificing my integrity, you said."

"But the vice presidency?" She stretched a hand out to him in automatic sympathy. He'd lost the vice presidency? The goal he'd gone after so ruthlessly? He was saying he'd given it up voluntarily? "I don't understand."

Josh shook his head, a rueful smile lighting his face. "The job was all-consuming. Work and more work and finally, I realized it would never be anything else."

"So you just quit?" She stared at him in confused disbelief.

"I handed in my resignation this morning," he told her, his gaze still watchful on her face, as if he had some huge stake in her reaction to his news. "I also made calls to some people I know. I think I'll be going into consulting."

"Consulting? But . . . but this vice presidency job is all you've ever wanted," she said, still not sure she understood.

"Maybe." He shrugged. "Or maybe I just never let myself consider *not* working for a large company, *not* being an overworked executive."

Katie stared at him in disbelief. "Josh!"

"That is . . . until you came along and pointed out to me how uncomfortable I'd grown the higher I climbed," he told her, his words low.

"Me?" she said, her disbelief shifting to shock.

"After our last conversation," he said with difficulty, "I've come to regret a lot of things. Like not telling you how much I love you. I really regret that."

She reached out for the counter again.

"You made me see that I could change my course, that I don't have to make a lot of money . . . just to ensure I never have to rely on anyone again. I know I can rely on you," he finished deliberately.

He loved her?

"But . . . my sister, my family, the Flanagan instability?"

Josh cleared his throat. "I also realized after you left that day how unfair I've been to you. From the first, I doubted you—but you never once let me down. You *didn't* bail out on me. You handled the studio. Handled the tough business situations I threw you into. If anything, I'm the one who failed you."

"No!" She reached out, taking his hand in hers. "You didn't. If it hadn't been for you, I wouldn't have learned to stay and face things. I would have given up on the studio, just like you said."

"But you didn't," he said with a smile. "You stuck with it, and it looks wonderful."

"I wanted to run," she confessed as he drew her into his arms. "So many times this last month, I just wanted to leave town."

God, he felt good, his embrace strong around her. Katie leaned her head on his shoulder, so happy it seemed the moment couldn't be real.

"You stayed," he said, kissing her.

"Yes." The word came out breathlessly.

"You have to know that I never loved your sister," he said abruptly. "I—I just fell for the thought of being a father, having a family."

"I know," she said tenderly, her arms tightening around him. He'd be a wonderful father.

"I love you. I want to be with you," he paused, his voice thick. "I want to have a family with you."

"Oh, Josh! I love you, too."

"I've realized how much my *heart* relies on you," he said unsteadily. "Without my even knowing it, I've come to love you more than life."

He dropped to his knee before her, her hand in his. "Will you marry me? I don't have a steady job, but I'll love you till I die."

"Yes!" she said, her voice choked with emotion. "Oh, yes, I'll marry you."

Drawing him up, Katie threw herself into his arms. "I think I've loved you all my life."